BEAUTIFUL GRAVITY

BEAUTIFUL GRAVITY

A NOVEL

BY

MARTIN HYATT

ANTIBOOKCLUB
NEW YORK

© 2016 Martin Hyatt

Cover design by John Gall

Book design by Will Petty

Published in 2016 by ANTIBOOKCLUB

ISBN 978-0-9975923-0-6

Library of Congress Control Number: 2016941641

Published in the United States of America

10 9 8 7 6 0 1 2 3 4 5

For Massimo.

For my family.

And for all those who never got out.

PROLOGUE

I have to tell the story of the fire. And about how I first learned what it was like to watch someone vanish. That's when I first learned that fire burns and even the cheapest stolen whiskey will get you drunk.

If I look hard enough, I can see it. I can go back to the beginning. I can go back to being six. I can go back and back until there is no back left for me to return to. 2007. 1997. 1987.

So now I'm going to tell you what I see when I see 1987. There is a rusted, green pickup truck on cinder blocks in a field of overgrown grass. It is January, thirty-eight degrees, yet this world is melting. The people in this world, on this piece of southern land, run from a shotgun house, which is burning to the ground. A dog barks from inside. Neighbors come to see, to watch the shadows of the inhabitants dance around the outside, waiting for the sound of a siren. A mother, my mother, wrings her hands, and then pulls at her hair as if to replace the pain of losing what she often refers to as "nothing like the house I dreamed of."

And there are the children, me being one of them, standing close to the truck. I know a terrible thing is happening but I find it fantastic. It has become a Saturday afternoon movie world where people cry louder and move faster before turning to stone for a few freeze-framed close-ups. This separation makes me feel safe.

My sister is next to me, crying like she understands the seriousness of it all. Like she's an adult or something and gets it all like a grown-up. And all that I want to say to her is, "Look at how high those flames are. They are so many colors."

The sirens come on strong, pierce my ears, and make my insides shake. I see my father talking to Uncle Phil from next door, and they are sharing something out of a bottle, my father nervously drinking as our house burns to the ground. Him doing what he usually does somehow makes everything seem like it's going to be all right. My mother is doing something else. She and my Aunt Cora are taking small plastic buckets, using the punctured garden hose to fill them, before tossing them onto the flames. In their nightgowns, they look like two skinny fairies, busily trying to sprinkle joy onto a house on fire.

I can feel the approaching fire trucks. In the distance, my aunt has stopped throwing water and is trying to get my mother to do the same. My mother is somewhere near the ground now, crying as my aunt holds onto her. I can tell she is crying hard because of the way she shakes. She raises a tired forefinger. I assume she's saying one more because my aunt lets go of her and allows her to get the bucket while the fire trucks pull up to save the unsalvageable. My sister runs toward them, thinks these men can do something, needs to be by them to feel safe. She tugs at my arm, but I don't go with her as she runs away to join the circle of safety. And my mother walks toward the house with the bucket. I know she wants to feel that she tried, that she did all she could to save the pictures of her children, the Evil Knievel cake she has made for my birthday tomorrow, the picture of her my sister painted in school yesterday. She tosses the water, walks to the fire. None of this shocks me. It all makes sense, fits in with the way my mother does things. It fits with the way I have caught her staring at the knives in the kitchen. Fits with the way I have seen her constricting and twisting herself in the rough ropes of the backyard tire-swing. Maybe that's why I don't gasp or cry or scream when I see my mother walk to the fire. She lets out a sigh. Her face becomes less tense, leaving her with a loose, content smile. She begins to melt before she reaches the fire, and she looks heavenly. And I notice how everything becomes silent, how I can't hear anything, not the others talking, not the crackling of the fire or the sound of windows breaking. All I hear is my heart beating, like I'm going to die as my mother turns to ashes.

My father and an uncle come over to me. "Where's your mama?" they ask.

"She went in," I say. My father looks at me as if I'm crazy. "She went inside the house." He turns to look at the house, as if he's going to be able to see her. "She's dead," I tell him. "Mama's dead now," I say as calmly as I've ever said anything. I don't feel like I know much, but I do know that my mother, even in her last moments, was determined to go home. Now we will always be able to say that she died on her way home.

My father stumbles away from me, as if I have done something wrong by telling him the truth. Then he calls out for help and runs drunkenly across the grass towards everybody else, as though it is going to do any good. He picks up my sister, and she clings to him. I stand by the truck, feeling that as long as I am near it, I'm as safe as they are.

None of it really matters now, not the firemen or the water or the faces of my relatives when they realize my mother is no longer. I don't expect any of them to come for me or to hold my hand. I don't care that I've been left alone, but I'm getting bored. All that is going to happen has already occurred. The credits can roll, the commercials can come on.

The door to the truck is jammed, but I pull until it opens. I have always been afraid of this truck, but because it has been with me for this night and has seen what I have seen, it is my new best friend. This truck will hold me. It smells like musty fake leather and some sort of alcohol. I don't know what kind. There is a bottle sticking out from the seat and I smell it and drink some of it. It's not the first time. I've been drunk before. I pour the little that is left onto the floorboard just to see if it will burn a hole in the floor or make the truck move.

I'm no longer paying attention to the scene outside. Behind this wheel, I'm thinking of other things that have nothing to do with houses on fire. I think about places where there is water. This is the moment I begin to think that if I can get close enough to the water, I will never have to worry about burning up.

They don't find me until the next morning. My aunt and father, with my sister trailing along, are talking. My father is angry and saying "boy" in that way that he does so often that it isn't scary anymore. My aunt is trying to calm him down. She smells as much like whiskey as him, says something like "poor little man."

My father actually puts his hand on my shoulder. But I don't need a hand on my shoulder. I want to laugh at them.

I want to tell them that they don't need to feel bad for me. In fact, they should be jealous. I feel sorry for them. Because they don't know where I've been in this truck. They don't know that last night I was kissed by movie stars, swam in the ocean, and ate steak in Paris served by a man in a bow tie. They don't know that I skied on mountains covered in snow, and that I had deep conversations with foreign-accented people who made me feel smart. Or that Waylon Jennings winked at me in a bar. They don't realize that I have been to California and back.

"You didn't drink this, did you, Boz?" Aunt Cora asks, grabbing the empty bottle. I shake my head. "You nearly scared us half to death," she says, as they sort of pull me out of the truck.

"I'm all right," I say. "I was just sleeping."

1

They say towns like this don't exist anymore, but I know that they do because I live here. Noxington is one of those towns where the big stores that sell everything and stay open all night have yet to be built. And it doesn't have those places where people sit at tiny computers drinking fancy coffees and eating expensive muffins. It doesn't have those restaurants where all the customers look like they spend a lot of money on clothes. There are places like that in towns forty or fifty miles away, in Mandeville and Slidell and, of course, New Orleans. But here we don't have that stuff, and sometimes when I can't sleep or when I'm bored, I want those things, that coffee, those computers, those clothes. But I stay here. I stay because Granddad needs me, and because in the past when I've tried to leave, I get sick. I get dizzy, and it's like I'm going to throw up, pass out, or die or something. I am not a good traveler. But one of these days, I'll leave. I'll relocate to a place where there are more people and more things. But for now I stay. Most of us in towns like this stay put. Besides, it's the only thing I know how to do well. I am excellent at staying.

But now I am turning thirty-six in this town where nothing ever happens. It can be said that the fire twenty-five-years ago was really something, certainly the biggest event of my life. But if you push something like the fire far enough back, it becomes less your personal history and simply general history. Something you can refer to the way you refer to a history book. People still talk about the fire much more than me, so it is like it is their event, something they have to carry around instead of me.

I am spending the morning of this birthday sitting in the window of the diner where I work. Birthdays are the sort of thing I like to keep a secret. And not only because I am getting old, but because I don't want anyone to feel sorry for me or to be sad about what I have not become. They blame what I have not achieved much more on the fire than I do. On this thirty-sixth birthday, I don't want to think about my classmates whose photographs I see in the morning papers, heading civic organizations, running for public office. They are doctors and lawyers now. And it seems as if they are all married. I see them smiling with one another in those black-and-white photographs. When viewed at just the right time on the right day, the normalcy of marriage seems right. It makes sense to be them.

There are no customers in the place. People get a late start on Sunday mornings. Not even my granddad, the owner, is around. He always goes fishing on Sundays. Jose, the cook, and G., the dishwasher, are out back smoking a number, so I take control of the brand new digital jukebox and put on some George Strait.

I look around the diner, which caters mostly to construction- and road-crew workers, hopped-up truck drivers, and to people who work at the courthouse about three miles up the road. And occasionally to people on the highway looking for a place to get a quick bite to eat as they travel to faraway places where it snows and smells green. This world, my world, is a muggy place full of grease and ketchup. It is a world of electronic jukeboxes and shaky folding tables where people grow old in a most expected way.

When your parents are dead, I guess you don't worry so much about becoming them. Instead, you spend your life wondering who it is you are supposed to be. In a town like Noxington, becoming yourself is never an option.

"Hey Boz, you want some of this?" G. yells from out back.

"No. Go ahead," I say, knowing that smoking pot will just make me more bored. G. and Jose smoke to turn working in the kitchen into a dream. But I have the natural ability to do this, to see everything as a dream. I also know from that fiery night I spent in the truck that you always wake up from dreams.

I can see them in the kitchen, wrestling with each other like two overgrown kids. They fight with affection, like lovers in a movie, tussling before a kiss. Sometimes they call each other names, but I know they love each other because I often see them back there looking around curiously, making sure the other one is still there.

Granddad comes in carrying some bags from the Sav-A-Center. Beneath his white beard and long, tasseled hair, his aging face is red from the heat. "Mornin' Boz," he says, heading to the kitchen.

Outside, the trucks are passing and replacing Alabama as the music of the moment. "Happy birthday," he says, coming back to the dining room and handing me one of the cheap, white, plastic bags. "It ain't much," he says, standing there waiting for me to open my gift.

It is a pack of ninety-nine-cent pens and a small white

envelope with a worn five-dollar bill stuffed inside. "Thanks," I say.

"I know you like to write," he says.

"Thanks," I say again. I had liked writing once, a long time ago, back when I'd stay up all night filling purple spiral notebooks with stories that I thought meant something. But now I'll just use the pens to take orders from ragged truck drivers and crooked judges.

"Kinda quiet this morning," he says, sitting at one of the tables, opening his newspaper.

"It's Sunday," I remind him. "They'll all come in later."

"Look at this, Boz. They ain't even gonna fix old Wymer Road and they want us to pay more taxes. Let this old man tell you something, they can't just go around asking for more money then not doing nothing with it. This is America. . ."

The trucks are farther and farther apart now. I sometimes spend hours wondering where they are going. And I don't understand why everyone else in this little town isn't spending their days with their noses pressed against windows, wondering the same thing.

2

When the diner is busy, like it is the following day, it is the only time I feel that Noxington's alive in the bustling way I often crave for it to be. All types of people, from lawyers and judges to construction workers, fill the ripped booths and talk loudly over each other like every word is going to change the world. Old Mel Carter, the high school football coach, is with his wife. He's looking handsome, even though he's still undergoing radiation for prostate cancer. He smiles more than the rest of the customers. And since he's a coach who is known to yell a lot both on and off the field, it is nice to hear him talking softly. I am still just as scared of him as I was in gym class. Back then, I thought he was either going to beat me up, rape me, or both.

"Judge Fitz wants his burger." Granddad says this to me as he passes by on his way to wipe down a table for four men who are helping build the new addition to the courthouse. I know that Judge Fitz wants his bacon cheeseburger with extra fries and a large iced tea with squeezed lemon. He wants this every day and expects us to know this and we do. But if, for whatever reason, maybe because our minds are briefly on something or somebody else, we forget his order, he glares at us like he'll put us behind steel bars.

The jukebox is loud and there is a lot of Hank Williams playing today. It is a relief, as the crowd usually gets stuck on the latest pop-country song that they'll forget about in a month. For a month or so, they'll play one certain song so many times that it almost begins to feel as imbedded in my brain as one of those hymns people still sing in church.

"Table four needs to order," Granddad says, even though I already know this. I am always nervous to take the orders from good-looking construction workers, afraid that they'll know that I really want them for something else.

G. is ringing the bell from the kitchen window. "Pick up," he says. "Food's gettin' cold." At times like this, with just Granddad and me serving, I go into this mental zone where I feel highly competent and mentally overloaded at the same time. This is how I manage to keep transporting the greasy food from the kitchen to the tables.

Just when the music changes from Hank Williams to one of those slow, sappy ballads whose artists' names are interchangeable, the judge starts glaring harder at me. He doesn't say anything, just sort of shrugs and looks at me, asking me where his food is by pointing at his placemat with his oversized fingers.

"This is the last time we're comin' here. It's ridiculous," says one of the ladies from the Clerk of Court's office. All of us know she and her co-workers will be back tomorrow.

I just keep moving, working, numbing myself with the chaos of the townspeople who are losing their minds over the desire for greasy food. This is the only time I feel safe being so different in this town. They know about my mother, my father, my reputation as a walking loner who is afraid to drive. Outside the world of the diner they give me strange looks, but inside I am in charge. I have a certain small power from noon until two, even if that power is simply filling what they perceive to be their malnourished bellies. Outside the diner, I am the odd aging man who they still see as kid. Inside, I am a fast-moving king of satisfaction.

At around one thirty, when the lunch rush starts to die down, I am standing by the jukebox and watching the remaining customers with their own vibrant chaos. The quieter it gets in here, the more I feel judged.

There are only a few customers scattered around the place now. And this is when I see them for the first time. They have come in quietly and have found a place in a corner booth. She is wearing sunglasses so big that they almost cover her entire face. Her cowboy hat doesn't swallow her the way some hats can overwhelm people. Her beauty is visible even though she seems to be trying to hide herself.

She is with this man who is wearing a blue baseball cap, a gray T-shirt, and khakis. He stares at her, then out the window as she looks at the menu. They are city beautiful. I don't know which cities they have been to, but those places have clearly rubbed off on them.

"How are y'all doing today?" I ask, finally having made my way to the table.

She pulls off her sunglasses and looks right through me. Her eyes are big and all made up with blue mascara. "Honey, I don't think we know what we want yet. Have you decided, Kyle?" She talks loud and soft at the same time. Her voice is raspy, like she is on the verge of losing it.

He shakes his head. "Can you bring me a Coke?" he says in a deep voice, the kind that sometimes shakes up a soft-spoken guy like me.

"Me too," she says. "I'll have a Coke. Two Cokes." She is looking at me like I have the answer to something more important than what's on the menu. "Do y'all have any soup?"

"Gumbo," I say.

"Kyle, you do love gumbo."

"Sure," he says. "Gumbo."

"Is it good?" she asks, leaning in closer.

"It's good," I tell them.

"Did you make it?"

"No. I can't cook. My granddad made it. He's a good cook."

"Well, hell, then we'll take two bowls of it. With a lot of crackers. Do y'all have those little crackers, you know those teeny tiny ones. What are they called?"

"Oyster crackers," the man says.

"We don't have those," I say. "Sorry."

"Then lots and lots of whatever kind of crackers you do have." She smiles at me, and I feel small in the same way I do when good-looking truck drivers come in and start talking to me. I feel scared. "I'm Catty," she says, extending her hand. "This is Kyle," she says, nodding towards her companion. Her hand is soft and warm and I don't really know how to hold it, so I just sort of take it and let go quickly.

"I'm Boz," I say softly. "Boz Matthews."

"I like that name," she says. "Almost as much as I like mine. Boz. Like Boz Scaggs. You probably don't even know who that is."

"'Lowdown.' It hit the top ten or something in 1976," I tell them.

They look at each other, surprised. He starts laughing.

She smiles at me. "Nice."

"I don't know why I know this stuff, I just do," I say apologetically. "I'm not good with dates. Not historical dates and stuff. But songs and movies and stuff, I usually know. Chart positions and years and all. . ."

"You sure you from around here?" she asks.

"Catty, leave him alone," Kyle says. "You're embarrassing him."

"No, he's not embarrassed. It's just that people around here don't usually know this sort of stuff."

"Well, he does," Kyle says strongly, taking off his baseball cap and lying it on the seat next to him.

"I'm from here," I say. "I live here. I mean, upstairs. I like music, that's all."

I hear the kitchen bell ringing, I hear someone asking for their check. I know that dirty dishes are piling up on tables, know that food is getting cold, and that everything I am supposed to be doing is not getting done. Still, I stay at their table.

"Do you know who I am?" she asks.

"I don't. . ." I say. "Are you from here?"

"He is from here," she says, pointing at Kyle. "Or was. I'm from a place like this. You know, there are so many of these nowhere towns in this great big wide old world."

"I like your cowboy hat," I manage to say.

"It's a cowgirl hat," she corrects me. "But thank you, Boz Matthews."

"It'll just be a few minutes," I say, as I walk away from their table a different person. I am shaken up. People don't usually look at me the way they just did. After all, I don't talk much to most people around here, and they don't talk to me.

I tried to explain it to Granddad once, this thing about not fitting in. "These people here. They don't really want me to be here. Or to be alive," I had told him.

"That's all in your head, Boz. You're more than thirty now, you've gotta outgrow that. You will outgrow that. Worrying about what people think."

Granted, I can slip into a paranoid state of mind as easily as, say, someone like my friend, Meg. But I know that they talk, not only about the way my father killed himself, or about how I have been raised, or about how my mother walked into a fire to die. It is in the way they take a second glance at me. When people pay extra attention to the way you pronounce certain words, or walk, or hold plates and set them on tables, it is something that you notice. They may not know that I want to sleep with the construction workers on table four, but they do know I am different.

I'm not delusional enough to think that they stay awake wondering about my strangeness or my uniqueness, but I do stay awake mulling over their suspicious glances. Still, I refuse to leave Granddad. And I still haven't shaken that childhood habit of fantasizing about glamorous, faraway places.

I bring out the gumbo to this table that has made me so scared that I can't look at them.

"This looks so good," Catty says.

The man, Kyle, looks up at me and meets my eyes with his own. And I stare.

"Thank you very much," he says, sounding unusually sincere about someone simply serving him a bowl of gumbo. He is the type of man who was probably once pretty, but now he looks handsomely beaten. He is not perfect. His dark hair has just a little gray above the ears. His almost-chiseled face has some lines along the forehead and beneath the eyes. He has lived. He is amazing to look at.

I want to just stay at this table and look at them. But my job is done so I walk away.

Jose is sitting down, breathing, glad the day is ending, probably dreaming of the things he told me about the day before. I don't disturb him. I let him stay in the Puerto Rico of his mind, with a beautiful wife and two smiling kids. Granddad is sitting with the man who supplies the second-rate ground meat for the place.

And me, I play some more Hank Williams. I am still calm for the day, though I know it will pass when the crowd disperses and the sun starts to sink. The lunch rush may be stressful, but it is the only thing that I can rely on happening each day.

Catty and Kyle are standing up from their booth. I haven't even brought them the check. I rush over to them, trying to total their check as I walk. They have left two twenty-dollar bills on the table. "That's too much money," I say.

"No, honey," she says. "That's the right amount."

They are slowly walking to the door. I don't want them to leave. I want to go with them. They have turned their backs to me. I feel lonely. He is walking with a slight confident limp, like he's been walking that way for a long time. She turns around one last time, as he continues on outside.

She walks over to me, tilts her head, and smiles. I want to be kissed by her right now. "Catty Mills," she says. 'Baby, It's Us.' Number one. 1987."

"Oh, God," I say, dropping my pen and feeling a little like this is isn't really happening. "I know that song."

"You take good care of yourself, Boz Matthews. In towns like these, people like you are real refreshing."

I want to say something more. I want to tell her that I love her song, how it used to be on the radio in the mornings before I went to school. Her voice, ravaged and ravishing, had risen above the attic fan in Granddad's house. But I can't bring myself to say this or anything else.

She is outside with him now. He is in the passenger seat of their red sporty car. I stand at the door, watch her get behind the wheel, and watch them drive away.

I've never seen anything like this around here. Only in my fantasies. I wonder if maybe I've gone a little crazy and maybe it hasn't happened at all. Maybe I'm just imagining them.

G. comes up behind me. "You still working here?" he asks. "Food's up."

"Did you see that?" I ask, still transfixed on the place where their car was parked.

"See what?"

"Them. Those two people who were sitting in that booth. The beautiful ones."

"Oh, that hot lady and that dude with the limp. Yeah, what about them?"

"Just making sure that I am not imagining stuff. You know, making sure that they were really here."

"Boz, you got some issues."

"Yeah, I do," I agree.

And slowly I turn and go to pick up the food that has probably already gotten cold.

3

There are peeling, pale, blue stairs in the back of the diner that lead up to the big room where I live. It isn't much of a place. Just a big room with a large aging mattress on the floor, gray and red milk crates I use for bookshelves and nightstands, a tiny black-and-white television, and a 1972 pawnshop stereo. The bathroom is off to the side, clean but stained with rust the way bathrooms in places along the highway grow old with color.

I have been living in this room for ten years. Before then, Granddad and I were sharing the house out on Hollander Road. At the time, I really wanted my own place. He was renting this out to a second cousin, Laura. It was just before she left to run off to Detroit with some military guy who she would later marry, divorce, then marry again. So I asked if I could live in the big room, which overlooks the highway. He said yes. "It seems like it might be the right thing, Boz."

In the beginning, it was something like paradise. I allowed myself to think things that I wouldn't have thought in my Granddad's house. There is something perfect about being alone in a place, free to listen to loud music at sundown.

I did have a few friends back in my twenties, mostly people I worked with. I would invite them up and we'd smoke pot and drink beer and cut up, and then they'd leave me alone to watch the dust particles float in the air of my sanctuary. We would talk about things and futures that we truly believed in. Most of us had missed our chances at college or becoming country music stars or running off to Hollywood, but we hoped for something. And when we got high, we'd talk in postcards, about the exotic ruins of Rome, the bluest mountains of Colorado, and big city jazz clubs where a young Chet Baker might lean on our shoulder. When we talked about these places and people, all high and hopeful, we believed anything could happen.

Mary Elizabeth, a motorcycle-riding woman with big red hair and a past that included prison and the near-murder of a second husband, would sit by me in the window and say that she was going to leave when the weather got better. She would always hang her legs out of the window, like she was about to jump and run away. It didn't matter what season it was, she was always going to leave during the next one. "When it warms up, I'm outta here," she'd say, smoking Camel Lights the whole time. "When it turns cold, I'm headin' to California," she'd continue. "Boz, how about you? You gonna come with me? We can work our fucking way out there. They's a lotta places along the road where we can wait tables. A lotta Ramadas between here and there."

"I can't leave Granddad just yet," I'd reply. We all had our reasons for staying.

"Well this town ain't for us," she'd say. "Give me another beer."

She did finally leave in the middle of a cold January rainstorm, proving that the weather actually had nothing to do with it. "I am going," she said. "Write to me, okay. We'll get fucked up together someplace where the weather's good."

They pulled her body from the ditch along Highway 59,

on the edge of Abita Springs, on a Sunday morning. It was around nine A.M., a time when she should have at least made it to Mississippi. She was drunk and riding through the storm when she supposedly dodged a deer and hit the pavement, cracking somewhat open before the motorcycle crushed her. I still hope that, if she was aware of any of it, she at least knew that she was in the process of finally going somewhere.

There are adjoining big-screened windows that cover almost an entire wall of my home. They allow me to sit and watch the trucks move past. The screens get dusty and turn brown, but they keep the bugs out and bring in what little bit of fresh air exists.

Another one of the waitresses of the nineties, Shelly, and I used to sit up here and hold hands like high school sweethearts. She was from a rich New Orleans family and was being rebellious for a couple of years. She'd dropped out of Tulane, moved to the poor side of the town, and had ended up working for Granddad.

The very thing that was different about Shelly was her desire to be different. She wouldn't eat what everyone else ate, a vegetarian in a diner where burgers were the most popular item. She refused to listen to mainstream radio except when she felt the urge to criticize the music. She dressed in black just so people would call her names and accuse her of being a witch. She did all of this so she could argue with them. "I'm just, like, not in synch with the rest of the world, Boz, I'm just different. I mean, I'm more different than you and you're pretty different. You know, I just. . . Oh, this town drives me crazy." She would go on like that for an hour at a time, and I loved it.

Loved to watch someone think every single thought out loud. Sometimes I would just watch her big red lips, arrogant sighs, and frustrated hand gestures, catching only a few words here and there. I suppose that I sometimes wanted to be like her, so open and honest, but I knew that she couldn't stay like that forever or she'd wear herself completely out.

I guess she did, because one day she announced that she had to return to the city because she said, "My parents are driving me crazy and I mean, I do think that they're so selfish and I mean, I deserve my trust fund." She'd said she'd come back and we'd fly somewhere special where we could get married and drink piña coladas.

Her photograph appeared a couple of years later in the *New Orleans Times Picayune*. Seeing her face made it seem as though it'd been a hundred years since we'd known one another. Her hair had grown out and she looked not unlike the insurance saleslady who stops by Granddad's to collect the monthly life insurance policy payment. She was standing next to the man she would marry, Geoffrey Keefer, of the Keefer family that owned a number of jewelry stores. But in the photograph she seemed more confident than I had ever remembered her. She didn't appear to be thinking about a million things at once. Her eyes, now tasteful due to the lack of black mascara, looked confident, like she had joined a new religion. I wonder if she had meant any of the things that she had said to me about what she dreamed about at night, about what she craved when she was wanting.

I never heard from her again.

I did have a male friend in my twenties. Noah was in

college, an LSU journalism student. Granddad hired him to wash dishes part-time. He wasn't like the other dishwashers Granddad hired. He was book smart, and from a well-to-do Mandeville family. Although he wasn't very tall, with short blonde hair, eyes green and big, he always looked determined and taller than he actually was. When he talked about something as simple as the weather, his eyes would become huge and intense, as if he were quoting Shakespeare or the Bible or something equally complicated. He washed the dishes with great force, as if doing something that he really cared about, something that mattered.

He'd bring me mixtapes with groups that I had never heard of, like Jane's Addiction, but sometimes he'd throw in George Strait or something else slow and beautiful. I read everything into these tapes, wondering what he meant by including them, assuming that the lyrics were directly from him to me. While I listened to them, I'd picture him in his white T-shirt, standing by the kitchen window of the diner, sipping iced tea with slow deliberation. He'd walk towards me and we'd kiss.

Finally, one night, he actually did come upstairs and we began to touch to Dwight Yoakam's *Buenos Noches From A Lonely Room*. The way he looked at me seriously when we pulled each other's pants down made me think he loved me. We'd roll around on the floor then jerk off, as if we had known each other for years. But when it was over, we wouldn't talk about it. In the beginning, in my mind, this was what loving was supposed to be like.

We did it a couple of times a month for nearly a year. By then I was thinking of him too much to even sleep. The more

I thought about him, the less he came around. Men just don't love men like that. Not around here.

I bought him a card for his college graduation but I didn't attend. I wasn't invited. It was a simple white card, blank inside, with a couple of birds on the front. I wrote "Good Luck" on the inside.

He didn't even come to pick up his final paycheck from Granddad. Soon after that, I'd see him on the news reporting on sports, and I watched him every night before I jerked off and went to sleep. Then one night I was up late with G. smoking a joint and forgot all about the news with Noah. I forgot about it the next night, too. I haven't watched him since.

These were the people of my twenties. These reckless pieces of life had somehow floated into my quiet world.

But there was one person in my twenties who wasn't like the rest of them. She's still around. Her name is Megan Richards. I call her Meg.

4

Meg is a year older than me and I have only seen her once or so over the past year. Meg's being at odds with so much of what Noxington believes has led her to live her life in and out of hospitals. Sometimes it will seem as though we've lost touch altogether, then she'll reappear just like that. And when she does, it's like she's never gone crazy at all.

I haven't seen her in over six months and the last time I heard, she had cut herself up pretty badly. Her mother told me about it at the diner one day. Meg, however, called me late one night, crying at first, almost lucid, then wound up screaming at the top of her lungs. At that time, she was in one of the newer hospitals in New Orleans, taking some new medication, which was supposedly helping her. There is always a brand new medication that is supposed to be the cure for her.

Meg's father, Preacher Richards, was the pastor of the United Pentecostal Church until Preacher Wilson took over last year. Meg has told me about her father secretly taking money from the Sunday collection bank to start his new real estate business in New Orleans. He has a new church there, and sells houses on the side. Now they have money and praise the lord in the big city.

Meg is the type of woman who, even in her twenties, continued to keep journals and write letters using colorful gel-markers, sprinkling them with glitter. "I like to see color," she would say, "it reminds me that I'm not colorblind like Aunt Cass. If more people around here took some painting classes at Noxington Community College, they'd stop all that old racist crap. They'd want the colors, the races to mix. The Ku Klux Klan, really, all they need is a good color theory class and they'd never hurt another soul."

Meg told me this the first time she came up to my apartment above the diner. This was back then. It was almost the new millennium. 1999. We were both twenty and I remembered her from high school because sometimes we would pass each other in the hallway, always alone because people were afraid of her and I was afraid of them. They thought we were strange. Me, because I couldn't quite find the right tree to hang out at during recess. The pot tree people weren't that interested in me, the hick tree people wanted to kick my ass because I read books. The religious tree people, well, they were the ones that I was scared of most. Perhaps because they were the group I could have given myself over to with the most ease.

But Meg was scary in a different way. Even in high school, she lived the sort of life that, if you followed closely enough, made reading most novels unnecessary. She has never been the talk of the town in the same way as scandalous Sally Posten, who quit school at fifteen and got arrested a few months later for dancing topless on a pole in front of the Buttery Fresh Doughnut Shop. She wasn't dangerous like Brian Brady, the smartest boy in my math class who flipped out late one night, and with his Walkman cranked to "All My Rowdy Friends" went through town shooting out all the streetlights.

Those events were horror stories with endings. Meg, on the other hand, is an ongoing drama. We keep waiting for her to not be alive anymore. But she always reappears, reminding us that even in a town where people die tragic deaths, stopping breathing is an art that some people just cannot master.

Two days after my thirty-sixth growing old birthday, she shows up once again. She comes in just after the lunch rush when I am sitting at the corner table near the fake dusty green palm tree Granddad thinks adds a touch of class to the place.

We have just closed for the day, and I am enjoying the silence so much that I don't even feel like turning on the jukebox. Jose and G. have gone to the Palmer trailer court to buy some pot, then are planning on watching some sporting event, football, I think. Granddad is out on Lake Ponchartrain fishing, although he always throws back everything he catches. And here I am, noticing how frightening I look in the soup spoons and knives, letting it get to me. I take my reflection in the curved, tarnished silverware to heart, believing that this is how I look.

Meg catches me looking at myself. "Boz Matthews," she says, then stops a moment and repeats my name like I don't hear her the first time. She comes over and hugs me, as if I am supposed to forgive her for not keeping in touch as much as I would like. I stay silent.

She is beautiful all days. She's always been so unlike other girls who have grown up as much in New Orleans as Noxington. Most of them once dreamed of mansions on the water and have ended up antidepressant-fueled, overweight, devil-obsessed, former prom queens.

Meg has never gotten any bigger in size or presence. Neither by weight gain nor by putting on severe makeup. She sits down on the table and we stare at each other nervously, both knowing the unease will take only a moment to pass.

She probably hasn't spent too much time on her hair, never trying to tame it. As she picks up a spoon and looks at her reflection, I realize that the most beautiful part of her is her soft, silky smooth, yellow-blonde hair that's crazy all over her head.

"Are you mad at me for not writing to you?" she asks.

"It doesn't matter."

She continues to make faces in the spoons, trying to amuse me, trying to get me to laugh. She has freckles and her face is always the shade of pink that people get when they're embarrassed. Maybe that's why she always looks a little uncomfortable.

"You can't use this silverware to look at yourself," she says. "You have to use expensive silverware. When Daddy took me to Commander's Palace, I looked at my reflection for the first time after I'd gotten out of Green Leaves. I almost liked what I saw."

"Green Leaves?"

"You know, the one in Slidell where they put me in that dark room for four days. Remember? I think I wrote you about it. Or did I call you from there? They had me so doped up, I can't remember."

"They all sort of run together."

"I know," she says. "I know. Boz, I ain't going back. Not this time."

"But last time you told me you liked the hospitals."

"You know, though." She leans in close to me. "I think I'm over meeting groups of strangers, making them family through group therapy and shared meals, then having it all taken away. Besides," she says, "in those places they won't let me kill myself. And when I feel like I want to, it's so intense. Daddy must feel like that when he just has to have a beer. I want to die when I want to die. That's why I'm not going back." She stands up and sort of sighs, and it seems at first as though she is going to start to do a strange dance. Instead, she lies down on one of the hard tables. "How's Granddad?"

"He's off fishin' right now. The rest of them are off getting high and stuff." She suddenly jumps up and pulls out a clear bag of multicolored jellybeans. She comes at me and puts a green one in my mouth. I hate jellybeans but have learned long ago to eat them for her.

"I'm not going away again, Boz," she says. "I can't."

She gets up and comes to feed me one last green jellybean. She walks around and hugs me from behind. "I think of you often, Boz. Your being alive and my desire for death are the only things that make me happy." From anyone else, this would seem like a twisted insult or a confused compliment. But with Meg, I know it means she loves me. That's why I pull on her hands a little before letting go.

I watch her walk through the sunset-filled room, thinking of how everyone, in addition to talking about her mental condition, feels compelled to talk about her weight. But when they call her names like "toothpick" or "rail," they aren't just being cruel, they're missing the point.

After all, Meg doesn't seem to need a body, and it doesn't seem to need her. Of course, she has limbs and she walks and sits and gets around the way most people do. But she does all of this in such a smooth, gliding fashion that you never hear her footsteps, even on the hardest of floors. She never jerks, never grabs or clasps anything. In another era, another place, this would have been called grace.

"Boz," she says, as she opens the door to leave. "You look nothing like you think you do in that silverware." I don't believe her.

I go upstairs to my humid room and listen to the night come on slowly.

I don't know what time I fall asleep, but when I do, I dream of Meg. And in the dream, she is a runner. Her body is stronger than I've ever seen a body be. She is in a pitch-black hospital room, but still I can see everything. And in the dream, she is running fast, then faster up the walls. So fast that she can run along the ceiling with the laws of gravity no longer applying to her.

5

G. is in jail. And since Granddad has spent the weekend at the fishing camp, he doesn't find out until the following Monday. And he is shaking with anger. Granddad doesn't appear bigger the way some people do when they get angry. Instead, Granddad seems to grow smaller, and he paces and shakes like someone with an exotic disease. I try to ignore him when he gets like this. Try to just refill the salt and pepper shakers on the tables, screwing and unscrewing the lids slowly just to make the task take longer. When Granddad is angry, I try to do everything slower, as if doing things at a slower pace will somehow calm him down.

He keeps looking at his watch. "It's six thirty. We open in half an hour, where is he? This old man's getting too stiff to get back there and do all that cookin'." Finally, he throws a dishtowel onto one of the window tables and takes a deep breath. "This town, it just ain't what it used to be. People used to stay on at their jobs. Keep their jobs. You wanted the one you had to last you a lifetime. Not these boys. They do everything they can to mess a man's business up." I worry about Granddad. Though he's still active, he's not been himself since his heart surgery two summers ago. I know that one day his heart will just give out, but I try my best not to think about those things. I like to think he'll be around forever.

I rush to the phone on the other side of the counter. As expected, it is G. "You gotta help me, man. That crazy bitch done put me in jail again. Says I was verbally abusive to her. Says I took the TV. It was my TV. Boz, man, I need your help."

I put the phone to my shoulder. "He needs somebody to go get him out."

Granddad sits still for a little longer, looking relieved and less perplexed. "That boy's gonna make me a mean person if he keeps this up," he says. Granddad's sighs are weak even when he loses his temper. I can hear G. on the other end talking loudly, wanting me back on the phone.

Granddad stands calmer now, not shaking at all. Now he is a man with a mission, knowing he is sturdy enough to do what is needed. "Well, I guess I better go down there. You boys just do the best you can until we get back with him."

Granddad pulls his blue cap over his head and walks out into the sun. When Granddad has a purpose, he always looks younger, like he knows he will live forever. He's bailed G. out of jail seven or eight times. G. is usually always guilty of whatever he is accused of. He is known to have beaten up a couple of girlfriends when they didn't love him anymore. Once, he got drunk and pissed somewhere on Bryant Street, then took off all his clothes and lay down on the cement before falling into some deep dream. It's not that beating up women sits well with Granddad or me, but, in my case, having someone violent on my side makes me feel safe.

Jose sits down, and I kick back with him, still sleepy from dreaming of Meg. He laughs loudly. "That man don't get mad much, but when he does, it's like his veins are going to pop. But he never gets loud."

Jose stops laughing, realizing that my mind is clearly somewhere else. "Say Boz, why do you stay here in this town? How come you ain't never left?"

I look out at Granddad, slowly climbing into his truck with his fishing boat still attached to the back. "Because of him. He took me when I was a boy. When my mother died he took me, that's what he did for me. You can't just leave someone that takes you at a time when there is nothing about you worth having."

"But shit, you could leave if you wanted to."

"The world is full of people that leave," I say. "I don't want to be like everybody else. There's something about staying. I don't know. What about you?"

"Sometimes, I dream of taking my girl and moving back to Puerto Rico and living on the same street where I grew up. Or maybe moving somewhere where the buildings are so tall they don't even seem like buildings." He looks stoned but is talking the talk I like to hear. "Don't you ever at least think about it?" he asks.

"Yeah. But I don't go because that ruins it. Maybe it's much better to dream of being someplace than to actually be there. When you're there, you have to live there and deal with it. But when you dream about it, you're just sort of hovering, high almost, like you can be there and then not there in a split second."

Jose laughs. "Boz, you ain't making no sense at all."

"I know," I say. "That's why I stay."

6

I have been lonely ever since I hit my thirties. I always thought that it would pass, but no matter who I am with or how many people I am around, I never feel like I'm truly with anyone but me. The more of a man I am supposed to become, the more of a boy I actually am. If Meg were around more, this might change.

One thing that keeps me going these days are the games I've created to make my room seem more like a home. I never go totally over the edge with this thinking or anything, but I sometimes pretend that I am not alone. I pretend that the place is haunted by someone beautiful I could have loved, and I am sure that they would have loved me back. Sometimes it is people like Robert Kennedy or Waylon Jennings. Last year, probably because I found a rare postcard of him at Family Dollar for ten cents, it was Kris Kristofferson from just after his *A Star is Born* days. It is rare, after he'd begun to look like he'd lived longer than anyone has ever lived. And he was beautiful even then. People talked about him after that like he was too old to look at. I love the post-pretty Kris more.

Lately, though, it's not him that I think about. Ever since I saw an old black-and-white Italian movie where people splash around in fountains and spend their mornings haunting castles, it's Marcello Mastroianni. I don't do completely insane things like talk to him or set a dinner table for two. It's just that when I sit in the window and watch the sun set, I'll put on one of his old movies, usually *La Dolce Vita*, and feel like we are watching the death of the day together. I know it is a little bizarre, and I sometimes wonder if I am going crazy. I don't want to end up in hospitals like Meg, so I just keep it to myself. But quite frankly, I don't see anything wrong with spending time with a ghost.

Sitting in the window, I wonder about Meg. Wonder whether G. is going to stay in jail. Wonder how people I know can live lives similar to mine and just accept it. Maybe I'll never really be fully alive just because I don't want to marry a woman, have kids, go to Bible College, or sell cars. Sometimes an ordinary thing can seem like the most extraordinary thing in the world. But not necessarily extraordinary enough to pursue.

I've also learned that if I put on music and turn the volume down on the television, I am surrounded by company. It makes me feel like I'm never completely alone. Carole King and Mastroianni mixed together make me feel like I have people like those friends I'd had in my twenties.

I can see the lights of The Tavern where I am sure Jose and G. are off to blow their entire paychecks. The smell of the dust is rising from the ground. It's this smell of summer heat that makes me think of the fairground and my father, and then I don't want to think at all.

The Tavern is tempting, but I know I'll drink too much and have to work tomorrow. I imagine my father must have spent the majority of his life feeling like this. So I walk past Mastroianni and Gina Lollobrigida, all grainy and precious, never more alive than on my old black-and-white television screen, and I pull my boots out of the closet. I sing "So Far

Away" out loud, trying to feel the lyrics like they are going to make me feel the way I felt back when I thought I had friends who would be around forever.

Granddad once said something to me about having "smart feet." In his case, and usually in mine, this means staying out of bars, not letting your feet take you to places where you'll lose part of yourself. But lately I have been spinning it around, thinking that smart feet might mean putting on boots and going out to meet some new people. Besides, Mastroianni isn't going anywhere. He'll always be at home waiting on screen.

Then I hear her voice. The sound of it nearly knocks me to the ground. Nobody has been in my apartment in months. And now here is someone. "I love Carole King," says a voice, intense and musical and beyond real.

I turn around to see her standing there. Tall and blonde and not wearing her cowgirl hat. She is glamorous and beautiful in a way that only women who have kissed men like Kris Kristofferson are.

"Catty Mills," she says. "Remember?" She is wearing a black skirt with high heels and a tight white blouse. But this is the kind of woman who also wears her voice as a piece of clothing. She could be wearing everything in the world or nothing at all, and still her voice would cover her and compliment her and keep her beautiful and cool, warm and stunning.

Since I never have guests anymore, I don't think to ask her to come in. Besides, when you live in a dump, you assume people know they can just enter. Still, she stands in the doorway, me being silent. All the while, I am wishing I would have combed my hair. I also fear that she can see right through my fascination with this Italian movie, seventies lite-rock, and everything else that makes me happy.

"Yes. I remember."

"Can I come in?"

"Yeah. Of course, come on in."

I stand by the window as still as I would be standing if Mastroianni had just climbed those old stairs to my place. She starts looking around in a familiar way with direct recognition.

"This reminds me of a studio I had in the East Village."

I'm still frozen. She could be one of those women you see in magazines selling lipstick, only older. Her blonde hair is wavy and down to her shoulders. She is an older version of those models Jose and G. constantly flip through magazines and salivate over. But there is something together about her, like she's made right, like she's from some town where people spend time taking care of how they look instead of daydreaming about Italian actors. Her eyes are almost turquoise, and she is the type of person who knows the answers to questions not yet asked. She seems to have it all figured out.

I don't know why I'm letting this woman, this strange, so-beautiful-it's-scary creature walk around my room like she belongs here. It's as if she's been here before, and she'll be here again. Though we've never met besides in the diner, she knows me. There aren't many people who can walk into someone else's room and make it seem like it is theirs and always was.

"I'm surprised you came up here," I say.

She laughs so honestly that it makes me want to hear it again. Even her laughter is in tune. I don't always know what sexy is in a woman. But her voice, with its raspiness, is sexy even to a confused young man like me. Her forceful gaze has sucked me into her the way only certain men in glossy magazines and on my old computer and Meg have done before.

"I was down there banging on the doorbell. And nobody came. We saw a light on and I remembered you said you lived up here. It's dead around here. We just drove back in. I did a show in Mississippi. You know, Kyle insisted on this mini-tour of the forgotten South, and I do mean mini, miniscule, as in playing very small shows at very small places. And now here we are in the middle of nowhere, and we're hungry. We can't find anything to eat."

I stand still, pleased to have a guest, but also wonder if I have crossed the Meg line and gone completely crazy, living in the movie of my mind. "You're very beautiful," I say. Not having had to be social in a while, I just blurt it out in a slight mumble.

She either hears such things a lot or she doesn't care because she ignores me and walks over to the window. She smells like one of those perfumes that make me think of the rest of the world, and I inhale deeply as she waves out the window and down below. "Kyle's down there waiting for me. I told him that I can't drive any further without eating anything. We were supposed to be going to stay in Meridian tonight, but I think we'll just stay at the old motel up the road."

I've never met anyone who has a voice that alternates this way. A voice from a woman who can either break a window or grow so soft that it sounds like a mere pinprick will cause her to bleed to death. I appreciate the softer side, but I am drawn to the rage in her voice.

"I'm sorry," I say, spooked, as she makes herself at home on my window ledge. "I can't cook. The diner's only open at lunch. The cooks are gone for the day."

"Can't you just throw something together? A sandwich? Anything?"

"My Granddad'd kill me."

"Well, for fuckssake!" she yells, rising from the window, behaving for a split second like one of my lunch customers. "Where the hell can a person eat in this little town? And I'm not talking fast food either. I need to sit down and relax a bit. We've been on and off the road around here for nearly two days! No decent cell phone signal to find anything."

"I'm sorry," I say. "There's The Tavern. They have some bar food."

"I don't wanna go to no bar! I don't want to make a meal out of chicken fingers. I grew up eating white trash food like that." She is starting to scare me, but when you are lonely, even the scariest people are sometimes welcome.

La Dolce Vita is playing out, the credits rolling, and side one of *Tapestry* is almost finished. "Well, I'm going to The Tavern," I say. "I was just getting ready to leave," I say.

"I'm sorry to have barged in on you like this. I thought maybe you'd know where we could get some food." She yells out the window, "I'll be down in a minute!"

But as she leaves, she runs her right hand across my record collection, across my Dwight Yoakam poster, across my gray-and-green-checkered bedspread, across my light-brown paneled wall. She seems to be feeling these things the same way someone touches something they've stored away in an attic or closet.

"Yeah. I lived in a place like this."

"I can't imagine you living in a dump like this," I say. "You know, I really like your song."

"Which one?"

I pause, because I only know one song by her. It was number one when I was a kid sleeping in a truck and dreaming of the ocean. "That one song."

"It's okay, honey. That's the only song anybody knows by me. All my other ones are better though."

"I'm sorry," I say. "I just don't know the other songs."

"You're young, Boz. You called this place a dump. This isn't a dump. A dump has trash in it." She looks directly at me, making me feel young again. "I don't see any trash in here. It's just grit, that's all."

She walks out the door in her black evening skirt and heels. "I'll walk you down," I say to her, telling her the steps aren't safe, that they are going to cave in at any time, but really I just want to be in her presence a while longer.

It is still beyond warm outside, and she doesn't hesitate to say, "Shit. It's hot." Near the bottom stairs, she asks, "Do you think that he would have been even more of a legend if he had died? Like Townes or Parsons?"

"Who?"

"Dwight Yoakam."

"Sometimes," I say, more forcefully than I'd said anything to her so far. "Sometimes I think that."

"Me too. But just sometimes," she agrees, practically aglow

in the dark.

I follow her to the shiny, red sports car. If I were one to know something about cars, I would know which kind it is.

I can barely see this other man, this Kyle, in the dark. But I want to see him in that way men like me are always curious to see men like Kyle in light and in darkness. A woman from nowhere has just barged into my private sanctuary and I don't mind at all.

"Kyle," she says, leading me over to the car. "This is Boz. Remember? He says there's nothing to eat around here."

I can barely see him in the dark, but can tell that he is wearing the kind of sunglasses I haven't seen since high school, those eighties sunglasses, the kind Tom Cruise wore in that movie. "Nice seeing you again." He says this all deep-voiced and bored, the way men who make me feel the need to protect myself speak.

"Remember, Kyle's originally from here," Catty says, looking at him.

He nods reluctantly, looks down, and then back up. "Do you know me from then?"

"Maybe," I say.

"Or maybe not," he says, shifting uncomfortably in his seat.

He is definitely not a stranger to Noxington, but I cannot tell him that. I remember him a little bit now. I remember people having talked about him. He's been away for years and had left in a way that has kept the town talking. But I remember him being a handsome young man when I was nothing but a boy.

"You can go twenty miles that way and there's a Denny's

and stuff. A few things. The town's called Bayard," I tell them.

"I know it," Kyle says. "Just hoped there was something new somewhere around here."

"Thanks, sugar," she says. "Boz, I don't see how someone who has so much life can live in such a dead fucking town."

The strangers drive away, some jazzy music with vocals I don't recognize blares from their car.

I am outside now, already dressed, and the record player is on repeat. Carole King will keep spinning and eventually welcome me home. So I start walking toward The Tavern.

7

The whole thing with Jose is that he's going to get caught up in another fight. When you grow up around people who fight, you can see it on their faces long before any punches are thrown, before anybody bleeds.

We've been sitting around The Tavern the way we usually do, and he's waiting for Connie Walden, Preacher Wilson's daughter. Connie has backslid more times than I've masturbated to Montgomery Clift or to Catherine Bach in old *Dukes* episodes, or, more recently, Marcello Mastroianni in *La Dolce Vita*. I like to see Mastroianni angry. I always get off on the scene where he gets into a fight with Gina Lollobrigida and throws her out of the car. It isn't a romantic scene, but it turns me on. Then there is that other scene that always gets me worked up. It's the Montgomery Clift scene in *A Place in the Sun* when Elizabeth Taylor touches his face. That movie before he was scarred, before the accident, before she pulled his teeth out of his throat.

Jose has already had too many shots of Jim Beam.

I have a shot with him, but he's already drunk, slurring his words, slapping me on the back. G.'s over at the pool table, looking like he doesn't have a care in the world. "He's gambling all his money away. Better not ask me for none next week," Jose says. Now that Granddad's gotten G. out of jail, it's Jose's turn to head for trouble.

"Business is bad, Boz," Hazel says to me. Hazel has a red mullet, and it is no secret that she has slept with more women than most of the men in town. But we never talk about it. I mean, you can't talk about that around here without someone getting their feelings hurt.

"Do you remember Kyle Thomas?" I ask her.

"Who doesn't?" she asks, pouring a shot of something pink for me, then for herself. "He surprised everybody, didn't he? He was the perfect Noxington boy. That was before he went away to Bible College and came back to take over after his daddy at the church." She finishes her shot and laughs.

"How do you know about him?"

"Everybody used to talk about him, they say he tried to kill somebody, then himself, then left town. Well, you know how people exaggerate. It happened in the church. He was engaged to Jenny Schmidt, you know the girl that disappeared a few years back? Well, they were the ideal couple, the prom king and queen of town, perfectly religious, perfect looking, well mannered. Perfect, perfect, perfect. . ."

"But who did he try to kill?"

"One day in church, nobody ever figured out why, although they all came up with their own stories, he walked down from the pulpit, walked over to his father on the front pew, and slugged him and then nearly choked him to death. Days later, he was in the hospital for one of those so-called accidental overdoses. He went to church a few Sundays after that. In the middle of the sermon he walked out and never came back. Ain't that some shit?"

"Never?"

"He just left town. Disappeared. Wasn't even around when Jenny died ten years later. Didn't even come to his mama's or his daddy's funerals."

"Is this really true?"

"That's the truth. I know because Jenny's sister and I used to be real thick, if you know what I mean. Why you asking about him?"

"I think I saw him earlier."

"Honey, I didn't make the drink that strong."

"Where did he go?"

"Some people say he finally did actually die of a drug overdose. Some say he went on to be a truck driver, but most everybody I know says he went off and became a professional wrestler. The real kind of fighter, not that WWE crap. I do know he was in Nashville for a while, wrote some hit songs."

"I think I did see him."

"Who knows?" she says. "Maybe he was like me. Just tough as nails. Speaking of which, you know some asshole came in here earlier, drunk, and insisted I give him a buyback, and when I wouldn't, he said, 'Fuck you, dyke,' and stormed out."

"I'm sorry, Hazel."

"Do you think people can see through us? Can they tell the way we are about love and such? About me?"

"It doesn't matter," I tell her. "Where is everybody?"

"Maybe they'll come later. But lately, they ain't been in much at all. You know how it is, people take turns, church, then bars, then church, then. . ."

"I know," I say, looking over at Connie who is talking to Jose. Jose isn't a bad-looking guy. In fact, I find him sexy at certain times when he smiles in his welcoming way. But Connie is known to like men with more money. Well, Noxington money anyways. Noxington money means bringing in a weekly minimum wage paycheck.

G. comes over. "Looks like they ain't gonna send me away," he says. "Some sorta technicality. I'm gonna stay a free man." He sounds a bit down tonight.

"If you stay outta trouble."

"Let me buy you a drink."

"No," I say at first, worrying that I am my father. Then I think better of it.

"Jose and Connie, they sure like each other," G. says.

"Let them be," says Hazel, mixing a batch of something sweet and sour she calls her SOS Bomb. While she is mixing it, an older man comes rushing through the front door and directly over to Connie. "Daddy!" she squeals.

The preacher is a strong man, older but thick-necked and strong-armed, and he takes the pool cue from Jose like it's a drinking straw. "Get outta here," he orders his daughter.

"No."

He tries to push her to the door but she clings to the bar. "Leave her alone," is all I hear Jose say.

I hear the stick hit Jose, but I don't see it. I have turned my head.

This is the pastor of the most popular church in town in a barroom brawl. Like me, Jose isn't a fighter. He holds on to the side of the pool table and rises slowly. As always, when he is nervous, he begins to talk in Spanish. I know that I am going to see Jose killed this night. But then something happens so quick and so brutal we can't stop it. It's one of those moments where you simply know that after blinking your eyes, life will never be the same again.

It is G. who sprints over and picks up another pool cue and begins to bring it down hard, then harder, on the preacher. As though he is playing a huge drum with a single stick. Hazel is calling the cops. "Slow Ride" by Foghat is playing. Connie is screaming as her father becomes nothing but a bloody pulp lying on the ground. Jose is in the corner sobbing, really crying, as though he is the one being killed.

The place has cleared out some, so I am the only one who can try to stop G. I walk over to him, afraid, though not of him. He turns to me and raises the stick high into the air, like I could be next. "Boz, you're always getting in the way."

That's when he turns and tries to finish off the preacher. The pool cue has gone from being like a drumstick to more of a kitchen knife. G. has tenderized the preacher.

Connie is nowhere in sight.

"G.," I say, "This time you're going to stay in jail."

"I know," he says, sitting down calmly, as Jose still sobs in the corner.

The sirens are outside. Hazel pours herself another drink. In Noxington, people often fight like this. People think nothing of pulling a gun or bludgeoning someone with a baseball bat. Maybe they think it is the way their lives are meant to be. Death hasn't surprised me since I was a child. I can usually see it coming. Maybe not on this night, or in this way, but I know that G. has death in his eyes.

I've never seen G. more at peace than when the cops walk in, and he calmly puts his hands behind his back. "I killed the motherfucker," he says. "Take me away."

I watch Jose at a nearby table staring blankly, like he's lost his own freedom.

"Are you okay? Do you wanna come back to my place?" I ask.

"I'll be all right. He did it for me."

Hazel is closing up, and on my way out I notice something that I haven't seen before. It is a poster on the back of the door: *Catty Mills: Live!*

8

I know I have to tell Granddad about what happened at the bar. This time there will be no getting G. off the hook. I walk home slowly along the dusty road with cars passing on each side.

I can't drive. I failed the driving test three times so I gave up. Nobody around here seems to understand it. Because I walk everywhere, I like to think at times that if I try hard enough, I can stop traffic. By just looking at an oncoming semitruck, I like to think it will stop. I like to think I'm that powerful. I don't know why I think this. But I truly believe that if I even go so far as to stand in the middle of the road and there is traffic barreling towards me, I will be fine. Certain things you just know about yourself.

Walking back home from The Tavern, cars continue to pass by me like always. But one slows down. It's that red car. That car with those two people. Catty and Kyle. They roll down the passenger window and look at me, through me. They are the kind of people who can see you even when you do not know they are watching.

"You scared me," I say.

"You need a ride?"

"No. Not tonight," I say. "I like to walk."

She lets out that laugh that I'm already in love with. I want him to take off his sunglasses. I want to see his eyes. I want them to be dark and as beautiful as the rest of him. And I want to hear the true story of his departure all those years ago.

They speed off, leaving me to return home to Carole King, but I think that tonight it's going to take more than her. As it has been a night of ghosts, I am surprised but not scared to see the light to my place is off, even though I know I left it on. On my way up the stairs, I notice how the music isn't playing. I imagine Chet Baker or Laura Nyro in the bed waiting for me. I smile at my own crazy thoughts. After all, I just watched a preacher get beaten nearly to death, and I am thinking of fucking Catty Mills.

The front door is ajar and I open it to see Meg on the floor. In the moonlight, she looks like a destroyed doll. She sprawls all twisted. It looks like she's been thrown from a car on the highway and landed in my bedroom.

"Meg!" I rush to her.

"Boz, don't try and stop it. I had no other place to go. It's what I want. Don't stop it. Let me bleed."

The fuzzy television screen lights up the room, illuminating what she has done to herself. She is naked and wrapped in my once-whitest sheet. A knife, the one Jose uses to cut up the chickens in the restaurant, is lying on the floor. "Meg, I'm taking you to a hospital."

She has made marks all over her body, becoming her own abstract painting. I am surprised that she lets me pull the sheet from around her. She lies there as most of the bleeding stops. But all up and down her arms and legs, she has sliced through her skin like she is trying to get some of whatever makes her so unhappy out. She isn't bleeding much now. She's cut herself in places that cause more pain than death. "Oh, Meg," I say, pulling her close.

"I'm not even sure why anymore, Boz," she says numbly, not shedding a tear. "Because I don't have anything else to do, I guess. What is a person supposed to do with their body if they don't cut it? That's what they do to animals, isn't it?"

"But you're not an animal."

"Oh yes, I am. They give me medicine, they watch me go mad, then they start over again." She wraps herself back in the sheet. "Please don't call an ambulance. They don't know me, they won't help me."

I don't know what to say to a doll that is bleeding and talking without anyone pulling a string. I know she won't die. People who are about to die lose the ability to blink. They take wide-eyed looks at their surroundings. Meg isn't doing that. "Do you want to die?" I ask her.

She lies back down. The knife is still beside her. "Boz?" she asks, picking it up, holding it close to her throat, then closer. "If I wanted to, would you let me?"

She is sitting up again, a welcome cool wind is blowing through the window. We both shiver. "Boz, tell me that you'd let me slash my throat and not call for help. It'd probably be too late anyways. But if I try to kill myself, won't you promise to not try and save me? When I decide to die, Boz, I mean, for real, will you let me? Please? Promise me that."

I am aware that killing herself, hurting herself, is crazy. But I've never seen anyone want anything more than Meg wants death.

"When it's really time, I won't stop you. But today's not it." For a brief moment, as the shiny knife touches her throat, I wonder if she'll ever do it. Meg has the gift for making you believe that she will die. This is even on nights when death is not in the room.

"If I slash my throat right now, will you let me bleed to death?"

I am silent at first. "Yes. If you really think this is the time. I'd let you die. I'd give you what you want."

She holds the knife there, and for a second or two, but not for very long, I believe that maybe she will really do it. But as calmly as she put the knife to her throat, she just as quickly throws the knife across the room. Granddad is going to have a fit when he can't find it in the morning. "Thank you, Boz. Nobody's ever offered me that before."

She hugs me close, her nipples touching mine. "Come here," I say, pulling her to the bed. "I'm going down to get some ointment and peroxide and stuff."

She is lying flat, staring straight at the ceiling. Dawn is coming upon us. Her beauty is soft and bright, even though she has tried to use a knife to make herself ugly. If anything, she looks more alive than before the cuttings. It is as though every time Meg tries to kill or hurt herself, she grows stronger, becomes more alive. If her goal is to disfigure herself, she has not succeeded. "I don't want to leave this, Boz," she says.

"Noxington?"

"No. Your place. Can I please stay with you awhile?" I start applying the salve to her wounds. "You know how crazy my mother makes me. And my father, I never see him. I didn't know real estate brokers worked so much. Mom seems less nuts when he's around, but he's never there, so she's always crazy." She pauses to catch her breath. "So can I?"

"Yes," I say. "You can stay with me."

Later in the night, with my shirt off and her completely naked, we sleep as close as two people can sleep together without being regular lovers.

9

Preacher Wilson isn't going to die. But since he is the preacher, hearing people talk, it's as though there has never been a brawl at The Tavern before. By comparison, when Malcolm Smith beat Jim Thomas to death before slashing his throat with a broken beer bottle, people talked about it in that way they talk about people who get what's coming to them. It was seen as though they'd been up to no good hanging out at a bar, so they got what they deserved.

Or there was the time when Janet Fallows walked into The Tavern and shot this pregnant woman her husband was having an affair with straight in the stomach. People seemed to act as though the woman deserved to be shot and that Janet deserved to go to prison for life. That time, I actually heard a customer say in the middle of the diner, "See. That's what God'll do."

However, since this is the preacher and because it is G. who has done it, the diner at twelve thirty is empty. The town has decided to blame Granddad for constantly getting G. out of jail. They've somehow decided to boycott the diner. Most of the people in this town think a lot and have conversations about how they feel about certain things, even if they never speak to one another about them. The town has always whispered about Granddad, about how he hires criminals to work for him, how it's wrong, and now they have their proof.

Granddad realizes what is going on when he sees the whole town walking and driving right past the diner and not stopping. When he comes out into the sun in his overalls and flannel shirt, greeting the people of Noxington, they look at him like he is contagious, carrying both death and darkness.

"How could you keep getting that criminal out? You just as responsible as him," says Judge Faust who stops in not to eat, but just to say that.

Granddad is trying to be tough, but I know he is hurt. When something really bothers Granddad, he pulls at the straps of his green suspenders like he is making sure they are still attached. He is doing that a lot today. "Things'll get back to normal," he says.

"Yeah," I agree, though I am not so sure, as I clean the windows and watch everyone pass us by.

"This old man's gonna go fishin', though," he says. "You boys can handle the place."

I've never seen my grandfather pull at his suspenders so much, not since he told me his version of the story of my mother's death. He looks like he's been cheated, like someone has stolen all his energy.

When Granddad leaves, I am standing in one of the booths cleaning the windows. Jose walks up behind me and sits down in the booth. He looks nervous, not unlike when we are really busy during a lunch shift. Sweat covers his forehead, and he starts flipping through a copy of *Sports Illustrated*. I can't tell if he's high or not, but I suppose he is.

I am mostly thinking of Meg. She is upstairs, all cut up, reluctantly breathing. She slept through most of last night, waking up only a few times. Each time she did, she sat straight up in the bed, mumbling words that weren't really words at all. Then she fell back against the bed and entered another deep sleep. She clung to me all night, mostly hugging my wrists, as though feeling my pulse with her fingertips somehow helped keep her calm.

Jose is nervously tapping his fingers on the table and shaking his right leg. "Boz, man. You gotta help me." I sit down across from him. "I'm gonna tell you something, Boz. Can you keep a secret?"

"I don't know."

"Come on, Boz. Please, man."

I stare at him with a trusting look, even though he can tell me anything.

"We leaving."

"Who?"

"Me and Connie. I got us two tickets to Florida. We going tonight. They going to want me as a witness, but we gotta get outta here or somebody around here will never let us see each other again."

"No. Forget it." Outside, the sky is darkening in the typical Noxington way, where it gets as black as early evening without ever raining.

"Boz, help me, man."

I get up, move to the other booth, and from the other window I watch people avoid the restaurant. "You are digging yourself in. The cops'll want to talk to you. Where will you stay?"

"Where I got family, I guess."

"What about Granddad? Who'll do the cooking?"

"What about me?" he asks loudly, standing up. "I've been slaving away here for years. I got ideas about things, too. You know that, Boz. I wanna leave." I've never seen him like this, all loud, his Spanish accent sounding sharper. He comes over to me; his face is very close to mine. "This is what I want you to do. If they ask where we're at, tell them we're in Texas."

"Why are you running when you ain't done anything?"

"I love somebody I'm not supposed to love. I'm scared if I stay they'll make it hard for us to be together. I want to be safe," he says.

The bell on the door rings and I know it's them because I can smell the freshness, the newness, the life. Catty Mills looks like she had her clothes made just for her. In her white silk shirt and dark jeans, she seems that she has forgotten what town she's in. Kyle is unlike other handsome men I've seen, including classic movie stars. Even Clift and Mastroianni. He looks better. Catty strides across the floor like it belongs to her and looks at the colorful images of the musicians on the jukebox. Kyle walks slowly with his usual slight limp. These two own every room or corner they inhabit.

"Is she always like this?" I ask Kyle.

"Like what?"

"I don't know, so up, so enegetic."

"You don't like it?"

"No, I do, I've just never, it's just, you know, different."

She starts singing in perfect harmony with Patty Loveless. She's moving around the electronic jukebox screen, alternately dancing and scanning the selections.

Kyle's slow-blinking eyes make him seem like he can't respond as quickly as he would like. He shakes his head. "Not Catty. She's different on different days. She's not always like this."

Jose is in the kitchen, pouting. I know what it's like to have crazy ideas, but I'm not sure Jose does, so I'm not sure if he'll be able to handle it. I want to go check on him, but can't tear myself apart from Kyle's conversation and Catty's duetting with Patty Loveless.

"I didn't mean to barge in on you like the other night, Boz. We were tired and hungry, though." She joins Kyle at the table. I am nervous as they look at the menu like it's a book I've written and want them to approve.

"How come you didn't let us give you a ride the other night?"

"Sometimes I prefer to walk."

They are both staring at me. I am trying to look at them long enough so they become real people to me. I have to find something wrong with them in order to not feel hideous. But when you are really taken with someone, it's hard to find faults so soon. I do manage to find some creases around her lips, some lines beneath his dark eyes. The more I stare, the more I want to do something to impress them. I want them to like me the way I had wanted some of those people in my twenties to like me. Until now, I'd been thinking I'd outgrown this trying to impress people thing. And now here it is again. Right now, all I can do to impress them is to take their order correctly.

"What type of bacon do you use?

"Catty," Kyle sighs. "Really? Why you gotta make it hard on the guy?"

"I'm not sure. I can bring the pack out here for you to look at."

Kyle looks at her, as if he's daring her to say another word.

"No, honey, that's okay. We are certainly back in the woods, though. Okay, we both want scrambled eggs and grits and biscuits and two mimosas." She senses my confusion and says, "Forget the mimosas. Two Coca-Colas with a glass of ice on the side will be fine," she says. "Right, Kyle? And can you just use the egg whites?" Catty sings out, "We try to be healthy."

I walk over to the kitchen where Jose is pouting, pulling off his apron. "I'm not doing it."

"You mean you can't make scrambled eggs with the whites only? Can you at least try?"

"Fuck, Boz. It's not the egg whites. Your fucking movie stars over there ain't got nothing to do with this. See, man, you weren't even listening to me earlier. I'm finished. I'm leaving."

"I was listening. Jose, you can't just quit."

"Boz, you been a good friend. But you know it's time for me to leave."

"Fuck!" I say, worrying about Granddad, about Jose, about how serving food is the only thing I can do for these strangers. Cooking is on my long list of things that I am not good at.

"Okay, tell you what. You make this order and I'll let you go. I'll lie for you."

He looks at me suspiciously. "Where am I going again?" he tests me.

"To Florida, but I'm saying you're going to Texas. Why didn't you just go? Why did you even tell me where you were going?"

"I wanted you to know I was okay. I know how you are, Boz. You worry about people. And that way you can tell Granddad I'm all right, too."

I pull him close. "Cook their food good," I say. "They're special."

"Who are they?"

"New people," I say. "Just cook."

As he turns to the stove, I make my way out the back door and up the rickety stairs to check on Meg. She's sitting in the window, still wrapped in the sheet. She's calm, as if she has been expecting me to arrive at just this moment. "Boz, I'm okay. I don't know why, but right now, I'm okay."

"I'm down there if you need me."

"Boz," she asks curiously and worried. "Boz, last night, did I talk in my sleep?"

"No," I lie.

She nods, happy to hear this, then turns to stare outside again.

When I get back downstairs, Jose has already brought them their food and is standing by the back door. I am angry because I think that maybe they would've seen something special in me when I served their food. Not that I think I am as magical as them or anything. But I just want them to see a little something in me that'll keep them from running away.

By the back door, I pull Jose close. He smells like a person who has to get out. I don't say anything else, just let him walk away into the burning world.

Catty and Kyle continue to eat and laugh. I watch their exotic, fucked up, disarming beauty from afar, all the while pretending not to notice.

"What do you do here at night?" Catty asks. "In this quiet, dead town?"

"Nothing, really," I gulp, clearing away their plates, preparing myself for their departure.

They are both watching me now, like they really see something. It makes me uncomfortable to not know why I've silenced them. I don't know what, but something about me has gotten their attention.

"Thank you, Boz," Kyle says, as his left hand shakes a little when he hands me a dirty fork.

Then I notice that they aren't looking at me anymore. It's Meg, she's come downstairs, all sheeted up, her wounds showing. "Who is this?" Catty asks.

"That's Meg." The plates grow heavy, my embarrassment weighs even more. I've never been ashamed of Meg until now.

Yet instead of being shocked or alarmed, they look at Meg, and smile politely. It's as though they're used to seeing cut up young women in stained sheets wandering around barefoot in diners. I watch them watch her, wanting them to return their attention to me, but I am amazed at how comfortable they are with her. There's recognition on their faces, a look of having seen this all before. This all makes some sort of sense to them.

10

Granddad's house is not beautiful. It is an old, peeling, grayish-white shotgun house where he's remained even though the diner has brought him enough money to buy better. From where I am on the road, I can see him in the distance picking up cans along the ditches. He always does this, perhaps an old habit from the days before he inherited the diner from my great Uncle Harry, his brother, and began to earn somewhat of a living. In the cloudy air that hangs over us, I do not know what to say to him. Lately, it's like I don't know what to say to anyone. But even when there is silence, I am usually never at a loss for words with Granddad.

Noxington is complicated like all small towns where most of the citizens go to the same church are complicated. I want to think the customers will return, but considering that G. has nearly killed the preacher of the United Pentecostal Church, I am unsure.

"I'm sorry," I say. "They'll come back."

He twists the top of his can-filled garbage bags and brings them to the cluttered porch. Granddad has a habit of keeping everything: old sofas, oscillating fans, birdcages. It all makes his place look much more rundown and dirty than it actually is. Perhaps these things make him feel as though he has some company.

"They'll come back," I repeat.

"Well, if they stay away, they stay away. Sometimes that's how things are meant to be." The way he sits in the weathered rocking chair, the way he rocks faster than usual, lets me know he doesn't really mean what he's saying. "We'll open tomorrow and see what happens," he says, watching the sky tease us with rain again.

I am sitting on the splintery steps. "Granddad. We can't open tomorrow. Jose quit. He left. We got no cook."

"Well I guess we have to find us another one then. Can you call the *News Banner* and put an ad in there? And we can put the sign in the window. That usually works."

He's calm about it all. This worries me. I want to see him get worked up, get angry in the way I know he can. "Doesn't it piss you off the way they can turn on you like this? In this town, everyone pretends to think alike," I say.

"You know, we don't talk about certain things. Because I know if we do, you'll end up drunk every night under a table at The Tavern. But let this old man tell you something. This town has turned on us before. When your mama died, nobody came to help us even though we didn't have a nickel. They just thought it was those crazy Matthews, crazy mainly meaning your daddy, fighting and bringing trouble to this quiet town. Then when he died…" A drip of rain hits the palm of my hand. "You don't want to hear about it, so I ain't gonna go into it too much, but when he killed himself, we were on the outside again. We never got no sympathy. We had to turn that diner around to get them to even talk to us. When Brother Keane was stealing money from the church, and I left the church because of it, they all wanted to turn on me then. Noxington is like any other town. Remember that. It's full of people who are approved of and those that are not."

"It doesn't matter, Granddad. We've managed to survive here. We have a life."

"If G. would have controlled himself a little..." He shakes his head in disbelief.

"Didn't you see it coming?"

"I never thought he'd keep hurting people. I thought he'd learn. I thought the only person he'd end up hurting was himself. And you can't really stop someone from doing that."

The cobwebs hang securely from the porch like they are going to stay there for eternity.

"Let this old man go watch the news."

"I worry about you, Granddad."

"You ain't gotta worry about me, young man. You gotta worry about you."

I follow him inside, through the screen door to where he sits in his recliner, and he grabs the remote so that he can have his watch of the evening news. The house is filled with old dust and books. It smells like burned-out bulbs and mildew. These are the smells of my youth.

In the hallway, I look at the framed photograph of my mother. She looks older than the thirty years she was in the picture. She has the same look as other women who become involved with men like my father. It is an ancient look, like a premature death is holding the camera.

I want to say the pictures of my mother are beautiful, but they aren't really. She was just another Noxington woman, growing old faster than people with money do, and always appearing in photographs to be looking for air.

The older pictures—the family photos of my mother,

grandmother, and grandfather—are ones where they hold smiles with their arms around each other. It's amazing just how much joy can be in a photograph.

The room I grew up in has nothing in it but an old stained ironing board and a sack of potatoes. The house isn't fancy, but to me it is. The old cuckoo clocks, the oil-colored still lifes, the random books are as important for me as the contents of any big city museum I am sure I'll ever go to.

"Sounds like rain," Granddad says. "Say, don't forget to call that newspaper."

"I won't."

I leave, still worried about Granddad. Maybe I am thinking too much, more worried about the restaurant than I need to be. But the people of Noxington and the diner are no longer friends, not even in that Southern way of falsely saying nice things to your face.

I walk through the dirt roads leading to the highway, noticing how a welcome kind of weather has taken over. It is one of those rare moments when it cools off in the middle of the afternoon and rain actually comes.

I only have about three-quarters of a mile to get back to the diner. Though I've always been fearless and not afraid of the big trucks, today I walk close to the ditches, stay close to the shoulder of the road. I wonder if Meg is still sitting in the window. She had seemed a bit better when I left.

The heavier rain shocks me at first, but then it begins to taste good, and I begin to enjoy the way it drips from my hair, down my face, onto my tongue. I fantasize that getting soaked will make me younger, more beautiful. During my daydream, a car pulls up.

"Get in," Catty yells from the driver's seat of the red car, which seems to keep showing up wherever I am. "Just get the fuck in. It's pouring."

"I prefer to walk," I yell over the thunder, over the falling water.

"People don't walk in the rain," Kyle says. "Are you even real?"

The car smells like new leather and Catty's expensive perfume. They are playing some country music from the early seventies, I think it's Merle Haggard. "Thanks," I tell them. "But I really do like the rain."

"So do we," Catty says. "But we don't like to walk in it."

I slip off my shoes and throw my legs across the seat. It all feels safe and new. I could keep riding like this happily for hours until we reach whatever destination they choose.

Catty zooms into the parking lot of the diner. "I have to pee," she announces.

So we all get out, the rain spilling down on us like we are being punished or blessed. They are yelling out in laughter as we get soaked. We just hold tight to one another other and run, and, once upstairs, Catty rushes into the bathroom. Meg has disappeared, but I know she'll be back because she's left her jellybeans. Since I don't have any clean towels, I hand Kyle a sheet. He dries himself off, and I try not to look as he moves his hands in the way that very macho men do when they are drying off, enjoying touching themselves more than they will ever admit. He hands me the sheet and I dry myself off, too, feeling closer to him because we've shared the same sheet.

"Now that's a rainstorm. Give me the towel," Catty demands. "Or that sheet, whatever it is. I am soaked, y'all."

We sit in various places in the room, move around, sometimes on the floor, sometimes in the window, listening to the rain and Todd Rundgren. "Boz," Kyle asks, seriously. "Why don't you drive? Do you know how? I mean everybody drives around here."

I pause for a moment and perhaps if we hadn't shared a wet sheet, perhaps if the room was not growing dark, I wouldn't have answered him.

"Because," I begin, as I lay flat on my back on the floor, "I am afraid of driving. When I was a kid, I spent a night in a truck and it did something to me. I tried once later on, but I almost killed the captain of the basketball team by crashing into his new car."

"Must be hard here without a car," Catty says, crawling on the floor beside me.

"People talk, make fun or whatever. They used to call me a fag and a sissy for not driving. I don't care about it anymore. It just makes me seem weird. I'm used to that around here."

Kyle is sitting in the window, carefully watching us lie on the floor. I want him to come to us, but it is ridiculous to think these strangers want to touch me in any way. "What happened in that truck, that night, when you were a kid?" Catty asks.

"A lot," I say.

"What?" she presses.

"Everything," I say.

Catty surprises me by taking my hand and placing it in

hers. "Honey, I know the feeling." She is looking at me with a stare that before now only Meg and some men have had the power to nail me with.

There is some thunder from outside and I shake a little, startled. That's when we stop looking at one another. When she reaches up and touches my hair, it doesn't give me that slight shiver that many others' touches have. I let her stroke my hair like I'm blind and deaf and really able to understand touch.

The silent room grows darker, more silent as night is coming on just like that.

"Everything slows down when it rains hard," Kyle says, surprising both Catty and me, standing there in the center in the room. He turns away after saying it, acting like he hasn't said anything at all.

I don't know how long Meg has been standing in the doorway. "Well, I'll tell you that this umbrella was not worth the forty dollars Mama paid at Dillard's. Just look at it." She is holding a dilapidated umbrella, a white one with orange ducks all over it and a brown wooden duck head for a handle. "It's dead," she says. "This duck is real dead." And for a moment it's like she's really lost something.

"Meg goes through a lot of umbrellas," I tell them.

"Just two this summer, Boz. Don't lie. And one was during Tropical Storm Artie." She comes in and sits down in the center of the room, just a bit damp.

I throw her the drying-off sheet, but she tosses it aside. "I like to air dry," she says.

I want to hear Kyle talk more, to hear him say something else. Or at least for him to get down on his hands and knees and let me watch him pray like he used to do in the church. Catty and I join Meg on the floor and lie there, as the room grows even darker. "So are y'all comin' to hear me sing at The Tavern?" Catty wonders.

"Okay," I say, staring at the ceiling. In this darkness, I am content.

"Just okay?" Catty sounds offended. "Okay?"

"Oh, yeah. I'm coming to hear you. It's not often we get to hear a real live star sing here," I tell her.

"Do you ever get tired of singing?" Meg asks.

"I'm pretty much tired of it all the time. Been tired of it almost since I started."

It is so dark now that we all appear to be nothing more than dark shadows. But because I've been paying such close attention, there is something already recognizable about them. I have already grown used to the way they move. The way they smell and the way they sigh. Kyle is sitting by the window, in a position that seems as though he is about to move in some direction, like he wants to be somewhere else, either closer, on the floor with us, or a million miles away.

"Well, I want y'all to come. I mean, I expect y'all to come," Catty says. "Kyle, haven't I have been talking about how I wanted them at my show?"

"I think they know that, Catty," he says, rising. "We should go now that it's cleared up," he says, now standing above us.

Catty sighs, sits up. "Okay, Kyle. Let's hit the road." She reaches out her left hand and he takes it, pulling her to her feet.

"Stay," I say, surprising myself.

"We can't, honey. We gotta get back to the motel and

change our clothes and stuff. Thanks, y'all," Catty says, running her fingers across our backs the same way she touched the things in my room the first time she entered it.

Kyle doesn't touch us, but he nervously comes close, like he's going to shake my hand. "Thank you for the shelter."

"I guess it's what shelters are for," I say.

They walk through the door as Meg and I rush to the window to see more of them. But they quickly speed off in the red car, leaving Meg and I in our own world, which now feels a little emptier.

"They're strange," Meg says as soon as the car is out of sight.

"We all are."

"I think I love them," she says.

"We all do," I say.

11

We sit across from each other. Meg is in my oversized sweater and my blue baseball cap.

She is so slim that it seems that if she moves the wrong way she will slip right out of the booth and onto the floor. Being small like this is what she wants. But she often covers herself with big men's shirts. If having no body at all were a choice, it would be her preference.

She sips her iced tea, which is all she ever drinks. Granddad brings over the plate of jambalaya. "Hope it's all right, and enough tomato."

"Look what I have here," Granddad says. "I found it in the attic. It was your mama's."

I take it slowly and then Meg holds it, rubbing the yellowed white sleeve. "Catty Mills. *Baby, It's Us and Other Hits.*" Now we can hear her one hit song from that one hit record. "I tried to listen to it online, but it kept buffering. Come upstairs with us Granddad, we'll listen to it."

"No, this old man's got dishes to wash."

Upstairs, I hope the music will be good, allowing us to hear her voice over and over again even when she's not around. We both sit on the bed, Meg having gotten so hot that she's now completely undressed. I get comfortable, propped on the pillows to listen. I haven't heard it in years.

The music begins, not quite like traditional country, more orchestral or something, but her voice finally comes on. "*It was you that walked in the door,*" she sings, as the scratchy record makes me feel like I am in the eighties. *"Baby, it's me who walks in the door, Baby it's me... Baby it's us..."* It's a good, maybe great, record. But it is even greater to us. Even the other songs, which weren't hits, sound perfect, and carry us away. It is beautiful to hear Catty filling my room, falling apart through music. Her voice sounds like whiskey and rain, like she's been up all night drinking bourbon and lemonade.

Meg and I just kept playing it. "Do you think she sounds like that now?" Meg asks.

"We'll find out."

We lay beside each other and fall asleep to Catty Mills's only hit album.

"Boz," the voice says, waking me. "She wants to see you." I open my eyes to see Kyle standing in the doorway. Had it been anyone but Kyle I would have been more startled.

"Why?"

"She's asking for you."

"Is something wrong?"

"Room six. Just go."

After listening to Catty's record all night, it's hard to think of her as being some other place. I don't say anything to Meg. I let her sleep.

"I can drive you."

"I'll walk it."

He looks a little tired, like sleep hasn't come to him this night.

"She wants you to bring Meg, too."

I pull on a gray T-shirt and jeans. With Meg barefoot in her light green summer dress, we march to the motel. This includes walking straight through the busiest section of the highway, where people honk and shout at us. We are both too excited to talk, not sure why we've been invited.

At the Star Motel, people usually rent rooms by the hour. Its brick exterior is weathered, and there is a bright red vacancy sign completely lit even when the sun is shining brightly.

Kyle is standing outside the door when we arrive. "Go on in," he tells us. "Go ahead. I'm going to wait out here." The room is dark and smells like bourbon and soap, like a barroom in a fancy department store. The bed is unmade in such a turbulent way that it makes me think it has been this way for a while. Beds in motel rooms, messy or not, hold the secrets of everyone who has ever slept in them.

Meg and I look around the room. There is a light from the bathroom. She hasn't heard us come in. But in the mirror, we see something I don't think we're supposed to. Catty is standing naked, slim, stunningly drunk, and looks half her age. But on the left side of her chest there is nothing but a scar. A mean, deep scar. Her left breast is not there. And in the mirror, her eyes drip tears, as though she has never seen herself before.

Meg and I look at each other and move backwards to the front door. I shrug, nervous, not knowing whether or not to leave. "Hey, kids," she says, coming out of the bathroom wearing a short, silky blue robe. "I didn't hear y'all come in."

We stare at her. "Kyle told us you wanted us here."

"Yeah," she says, pouring another Scotch from the bottle. "Want some?"

I don't need any. I am already drunk from her. She crawls

into the bed and covers up, her hand grasping the glass. "I'm having it bad today," she says. "I don't know how I'll sing at The Tavern. I don't usually get like this in small towns. In Vegas, yeah. But not here. Not in towns like this."

She pats the bed for us to sit by her on the cheap, rough comforter tangled with the fading, flower-patterned sheets. "I was just so scared this morning. I couldn't leave the room. That's when I asked Kyle to come and get you two."

"We like your old album," Meg says.

"You're a doll, but honey, do you know how much I hate that one song? Kyle was an angel for writing that one. But what a curse to have only one. Standing up there year after year, saying 'I want to thank y'all all for making this one number one.' And everybody clapping and pretending that they don't know that I'm washed up. But they do, and so do I. I've been washed up for most of my life." She takes a long, impressive drink of Scotch. "Y'all were sweet to come. I'm scared. Like nobody's gonna cut me no slack."

"Why do you care more about Noxington than a big city?" I ask.

"I grew up in a small town. Charlotte, Texas. They hated me and judged me and ran me out of there. I let them get to me. I always go back to small towns like I'm bigger now, and better. But I still feel like I'm dying in most of them." She shakes her head after taking a gulp of the strong whiskey. "So it just brings up all that stuff. All that shit that makes me crazy and unable to get out of bed. But sometimes, ever since the surgery, I feel it in every town. At least in the big cities, they sometimes pay attention and know the other songs too."

"Catty, you'll do fine here," I tell her. "The Tavern'll love you."

"Really? Come here." Again, she motions for us to crawl beside her on the bed. I wonder about Kyle outside. "The year I sang that song on the CMAs, it was up for everything. Kyle was up for songwriter, I was up for best new artist and best female vocalist. That usually doesn't happen to a new artist."

"Did you win?" Meg asks, then fades a bit, like she shouldn't have asked.

"No. That's when I knew. That song was going to be the only one."

"The only one?" I wonder.

"The only one they'd let me take that far. The only big one. They don't like women like me in Nashville."

"Like you?" I ask, as I become more relaxed on the bed.

"You know, you can be tough, but only so much, you still have to have a husband, and pretend to be a good country girl. I never was. In case you haven't noticed, I'm not a good girl, honey. If I would have known back then that marrying Kyle, pretending to be a bit more dumb, pretending to be softer, would have given me a couple of more hits, I would have done it." She takes another drink, and the more she drinks, the more sense she makes. "Nowadays they call it selling out. I didn't know I wasn't selling out. I thought that by just telling the truth, and by being myself, like the boys were doing, you know, Waylon, Cash, Willie, it would pay off."

"But still, that song, that album, is beautiful," I say. "It's considered a classic. 'A seminal record,' Granddad called it."

"Yeah," she said. "Everybody copied that sound. They changed it just enough to get airplay."

"At least you were yourself."

"I know." She slams the bottle down on the bed, a bit of the whiskey sloshes out and hits my chin. I don't bother to lick it or wipe it away. I let it stay there, glistening in the dark. "Listen to me, I sound bitter. Kyle says I am. I don't mean to be. I just wanted more. I worked hard. I deserved more."

"There's still time."

"Oh, Boz," she laughs. "When you are a fifty-something-year-old woman who had one hit record and are tougher than most men in Nashville, you are a period piece. I am a difficult relic."

"Most people," Meg says, lying beside her, "never have one hit record. Never even make a single record."

"Gratitude. That's the AA bullshit they tried to shove down my throat at Betty Ford in the eighties."

Even in her drunken and disheveled state, she is electrifying to look at. Like there is a high-voltage outlet she's plugged into. Even with her laid out and sickly, she radiates heat. In the dark it is hard to tell, but when I look into her eyes, I have to admit she is looking at Meg and me like she wants to do more than just talk.

"I think you're both beautiful," she says. "You two are something to be grateful for. Boz, take off your shirt and lay beside me for a while. Meg, take off your dress."

She gives us these orders like she knows we'll follow them. And we do.

I don't know what is going to happen and I am nervous because, after all, she is a woman. And as much as I feel the heat rising from the sheets, I am still thinking of Kyle.

Gently, safely, her hand strokes my chest. I watch her and Meg touch each other as though they have never touched flesh, not even their own before. Their hands are moving slowly, then quickly, then slowly again all over each other.

"I'm not perfect," Catty says.

"Thank God," I tell her as she pulls off her robe, revealing her scar that stands out as she and Meg touch each other down below. Even though it is a scar that matters, the type that can make even tough women like Catty cry, it's like Meg is making it disappear.

I keep thinking of Kyle outside, all sweaty and hot and tired, and wonder why he isn't in the room with us. These two women are loving each other in a way that I can tell is tender by the soft noises they are making. I want to join in, but I don't know how, don't want to, knowing that this moment of satisfaction is theirs. When people are touching each other in just the right way, you don't want to mess it up. I creep from the bed, pull on my shirt, and go outside.

Kyle is punching a boxing bag he's hung up under a tree near the motel porch. Watching him hit the bag is rough and harsh, so different from Catty and Meg's lovemaking. "I left," I say. "I think she's getting what she brought us here for."

"Why aren't you in there?"

"That's not the way I love," I say.

He is punching the bag and breathing hard. "She sometimes gets like that, wanting company from new friends."

"And you don't care?"

"What's there to care about? As long as it makes her feel better."

"Do you miss it?" I ask.

"Catty's body or boxing?"

"Boxing. Can you ever do it again?"

"No," he says. "And yes, I miss it. It's got to do with a blow to the head I got in Memphis. That's why I shake sometimes. But yeah, I used to be a real good boxer."

I watch as he pounds away at the bag. "It meant a lot to Catty to see you this morning. When she gets fixated on somebody, she doesn't leave them alone. It doesn't happen often, but when it does…"

"When's the last time it happened?" I ask, wondering if he just goes around finding people for Catty to sleep with.

"In 1982. With me," he says. "She wanted me to make her feel like she was going to be okay."

"And did you?"

"As much as I could. When Catty crashes, sometimes not even the people she craves can calm her down."

It is unsettling to watch him beat this bag, hitting it with such force. I want him to be touching me like this, even if it hurts. "I'm going to head home," I say. I have to get away from here for fear that I might do something stupid, or say something I don't want him to know, something too real. The truth.

"See you later, Boz. Thanks again."

Of course, I'm angry with him for just letting me walk away like this without so much as shaking my hand or touching me. I want his hands on me. I want his touch, even if it means him busting me in the mouth or something like that.

12

I become somewhat of a spy. I am good at it. The next day, nobody knows that I watch as Kyle goes into the church looking like a rugged angel. Nobody will know that I watch him from the back of the church, as he gets down on his hands and knees. Nobody will ever know that I see him cry in a way that men like him are not supposed to. I see him break without him knowing it.

Later that night, the wind is blowing through the room and makes the edges of the sheets flutter. I love the wind, and we haven't gotten a lot of it lately. Meg is pressed close to me. I get up, wake her. "I'll be back," I say, "I'm going for a walk."

She looks at me like she is going to question it, but doesn't. Instead, she falls right back to sleep, curling into a position that makes her look more like the Meg of ten years ago.

After her encounter with Catty, she spent the day in New Orleans with her mother who wanted to take her shopping. She'd returned after I'd fallen asleep, so we still have not discussed what happened. I want to know every detail and am tempted to wake her, but the wind feels too good.

I throw on some clothes, my usual—a white T-shirt and worn jeans. I want to be like Meg who loves to walk barefoot, but I know that I won't be lucky like her. I know that I'll end up cutting a foot on some piece of broken glass and bleed to death on the side of the highway. As much as Meg prances around town with no shoes on, I have never known of her cutting her feet.

I take another look at her, knowing that the red marks that have been bleeding cuts will soon become healed, white-lined memories. And in the room this night, they seem like natural parts of her flesh, like she has been born with them.

I leave to be in the wind, but I also have a mission. Often, I'll go for midnight walks, but usually it is when the ghosts of my room or my mind won't let me sleep. Tonight, it is because I want to feel the wind, want to walk up the highway, want to see them. Want to see Catty and Kyle. Need to.

Determined and alone, I feel powerful. Changes in the weather do this to me, especially breezes. During tropical storms and hurricanes, I feel like a superhero, like I am stronger than nature itself. The wind makes me brave, makes me feel like I have some powers that most humans don't have.

As I walk along the side of the road, every time a big truck passes, I feel stronger than it is. Perhaps this is why I begin to walk down the middle of the road, as usual believing that by simply staring at a vehicle I can stop it dead in its tracks.

But when a truck does breeze honkingly by me, I stop for a moment, losing myself in the force of the wind brought by its passing. I am on the side of the road when another truck, this one carrying vegetable oil, stops. "Want a lift?" The driver is almost good-looking, and I would have been interested if I didn't have Catty and Kyle on the brain.

"No. I already have one." I keep walking along the side of the road as the wind whirls around me, allowing me to pretend that it is the beginning of autumn. That is when everything always feels beyond good for about a month.

The motel sign is missing its red, flashing M and I wonder

if, like the old diner, like the town itself, this place will continue to crumble until one day it is no more.

It's growing less windy as I near the motel with its shamrock-shaped pool no bigger than if you put several claw-foot bathtubs like mine together. John Swaggerty, the owner, used to let me swim here when I wanted. But ever since he had a heart attack and his son took over, there's been no more swimming in the small pool for me.

Past the rusted, chain-linked pool fence, I look at the motel and at the tree with Kyle's punching bag. Their red car is the only one in the parking lot. I see the row of eight rooms and know that I have to simply go knock and the rest will work out. I have no idea what I am expecting to happen once I'm there, or even what I want to occur. The wind simply takes me places.

Walking to their door, I feel less of a superhero and more of my regular self. Knocking has never seemed like such a job until now. Even my hands are feeling heavy in a way they shouldn't feel when you simply have to knock on a door.

Their light is on. I know this because of the slight crack in the opening of their thick, brown-and-orange striped curtains. Their window is open, though the curtains are almost completely drawn and the air conditioning is on. I walk over and look, not expecting to see more than a single sliver of light. But standing just the right way, I can see much more. I can see them.

The television is turned to late night CNN, though neither of them is watching it. Instead, Kyle is in an old yellow vinyl chair and Catty is sitting at the bottom edge of the bed. Catty is wearing a silk robe all open, her lone breast hanging out, her beautiful body in plain view. And Kyle is wearing a pair of striped boxer shorts and nothing else. They both have tough bodies, bodies that can give and take a lot. Their bodies must get intense workouts from the fast-paced lives they lead. I get hard. I think about Catty and Meg together, wishing I would have touched Catty more. Wish I would have run my tongue down her scar, down her belly, to that sweet hot spot between her legs. I wish I would have made her feel how much I love her by controlling her voice with my tongue, listening to the beauty of her coming. Maybe I shouldn't have left it all up to Meg, because now I really want to taste Catty in that way too.

And they are talking. Just like when I saw Kyle praying, I want to hear every word but can't quite. I can catch full glimpses of them, like tiny drawings or photos in one of those books where you flip through the pages real fast, setting a scene in motion.

Kyle looks troubled. His once perfect, now somewhat lean but slightly meatier body is slung into the chair. I want badly to run my hands over the gray and black hairs on his chest. But he is strained, on the verge of breaking in some way. Catty looks good, seeming fully in charge for now and quite sober, as she drinks something the color of bourbon from a glass.

Catty begins to rub her arms, then gets up and walks over to the window, turning off the air conditioner. The newscaster is talking about Internet dating, but I don't know what Catty and Kyle have been talking about. Now, with the air conditioner off, I can hear them clearly. "It's cooling off anyways," she says. "That nice breeze will work a while. Another cheap room with the best and worst air conditioning in the world," she says.

"I nearly froze last night. It is either freezing or blazing hot in here."

"We have been in worse rooms," he says. "Much worse."

"Besides, I think you left the window open."

"Oh, honey, I ain't complainin', just sayin' how these cheap places always have really strong air conditioning. Tonight we might only need to leave the window open if that breeze keeps up." She returns to the edge of the bed and sips her drink. "Go ahead, finish what you were saying before I got up."

"What was I saying?" he asks.

"About being back here."

"It's just fuckin' strange." Kyle's words are harsh, but his voice is softer, gentler than I remember. "Especially because they all have stories about me. They've created their own versions of me."

"Oh, that small-town crap. I know what that's like. Even when I go back home, they think they all have ideas about who I am or was or could have been or could be..." She pauses for a moment. "Sorry, honey. We're talkin' about you for a change. You know how I am, getting carried away talking about myself."

Kyle picks up the remote and turns off the television.

She laughs softly. "I admit that I get carried away talking about me. But I'm getting better at it."

He grins at her and shakes his head.

"We can leave, you know. I can cancel this show. After all, it ain't much money. And I thought you wanted to come back here. That's why we booked it," Catty tells him.

"I know that," he says. "I went to my father's grave today

and thought about how it went so wrong and how it would have all been different if I would have stayed. If I could have gone along with everything this town had planned for me. I was a star in this town. Shit, Catty, you know all this, how it is. I was a golden boy in this town."

"And I know you hated it."

"Yeah, because it doesn't make a difference if you're the star of the wrestlin' team in Noxington, or a star writer in Nashville, or just the star of whatever it is you do every day, it never feels the way it looks."

"Come here, baby," she moves toward him. "This place doesn't matter. Nashville, okay, Los Angeles, okay. But this is Noxington, Kyle."

"Exactly."

"You feel like you failed."

"That's the problem. I don't even feel like a failure. I wanted to be a great boxer, I wanted to be someone who could write songs for my whole life. I wanted to be someone who could touch people and make love to them the way you do."

I am comfortable now, in my place outside. I can hear the tears in their throats, can see the longing on their midsections. I feel the need to sneeze, but stifle it, knowing that being found snooping like this will ruin everything.

"Regrets eat us up anyway," Catty tells him. "You are the one that told me that. I ain't never seen you like this, baby," she says. "You're usually like 'Fuck everybody, fuck the world,' and now it's really getting to you. Do you mean you wanted driving a truck or being a preacher to be your claim to fame?"

There must be at least two minutes of silence before he replies: "I can't even drive a truck." Just when I rise and see that they are still in their same places, Kyle speaks again. "This kills," he says.

Catty eyes grow big, her mouth half-agape. I think she's going to drop her glass. "What did you say?"

"You heard me."

"What kills?"

"It kills me to be back in a place I never wanted to see again and have it feel it's my own and, at that same time, like I never existed here at all. People around here drive trucks. I can't do that. They pray well, they speak in tongues, they are settled. And to know that all those people that I left behind are way too dead for me to talk to. And my leg's all fucked up..." He lets out a deep breath, and shakes his head. "I'm a cripple, and I feel like I'm goin' crazy."

"Come here," she says. She sits on the edge of the bed.

He stays put, but begins to focus on her gaze, his face becoming looser, relieved, as if when she's not around he doesn't have any place to go at all.

"You've done a lot, Kyle. A lot of amazing things. You were a Noxington star and managed to break away from this fucking place. You made me a country star. You fought with the best lightweight boxers in the country. You wrote beautiful music. Even the lesser-known songs ended up being recorded by some big names."

"I could have done better."

"Well, fuck, Kyle, we all could have. Come here," she says again.

This time, he slides out of the chair and crawls across the floor and in between her legs, each sigh he takes releases some of what is troubling him. She puts her right hand on his head, runs her fingers through his hair the way she did with me. She stops only to take a sip from her glass, which she has not let go of. And he rests there, growing calmer, staring blankly at the empty wall. With her hands still all over his hair, she says, "What do you need, Kyle?"

"I don't know," he says, his voice breaking. I watch his face as the tears build. "I really don't know."

"People should try for nothing less than everything," she says, her voice softening. "There's still time." They both look comfortable in what appears to be a very familiar, interlocked position. They are at ease in a way that I have never been, to the point where it seems as though this occurs every night with them. "It'll be okay, Kyle. It's going to be fine."

I peer a while longer, feeling both captivated and guilty for viewing such privacy. And I want to see what will happen next, but I can tell from the way she's touching him, the way he clutches her arms and legs in desperation, that nothing sexual is going to happen. If I come back tomorrow morning, I am sure I'll find them in the same position.

I know that I have just seen something beautiful that I had no right to see, have listened to things I had no right to right to hear. And yet I feel like without seeing them like this, I would have never known that they were real human people. I want to blame it on the wind, but that stopped blowing long ago. The only thing I can do now is run home. And along the way, I keep thinking of them cradled on the floor, holding each other, hungry and safe.

When I finally climb into my bed, I am so hard that I try to wake Meg to fool around. When she doesn't respond, I turn over and stare at the ceiling and think of what I have seen tonight. I shoot harder than I have since my twenties, then I hold Meg like I've not held anyone in a long time.

13

Granddad is in the kitchen running a nearly empty rack through the dishwasher.

I sit down on the counter and watch him closely. And I'm not sure if it is the unusual events that have taken place over the past couple of days, I think maybe it's the way I am fixated on Kyle punching that bag, or Catty holding him between her legs, but for some reason, Granddad looks different. He is dressed the same, suspenders and all, no paler than usual, but it's in the way he moves. Even though he still moves fast, I notice how much less deliberate he is when he wipes the counter or sweeps the floor. It is as though he doesn't care the way he used to, even two weeks earlier it mattered more.

"Well, that Jenkins boy is going to start tomorrow. He ain't had no run-ins with the law, as far as I know."

I don't say anything. I am too busy noticing how different he looks, how something about him has changed. It is as though, while he is still Granddad, someone has taken away the part of him that cares about empty cans and clean counters. I know that having no business would get to him.

Later, in bed, I think of Catty and play her song a couple of times. I am lonely, waiting for Meg to come home. I am jealous and ashamed that I couldn't touch Catty, fuck Catty, the way Meg did. I imagine them taking Meg out of this town to some city that has lights that stay on all night. Cities where they belong. Even though I advised Meg not to, I have started thinking about them too much myself.

I keep tossing and turning in my underwear, listening to online radio shows to cure the loneliness. And I'm troubled about Granddad. I try to push it into the back of my mind, but Granddad's face keeps coming back.

I have never considered myself psychic, though I believe some people are. I don't know what is going to happen with Meg and Catty or Kyle or the diner. But I do know one thing. I know that I will find my grandfather dead in his bed in the morning, his hands across his chest, his mouth wide open, as if to say "goodbye."

When Meg comes home, I don't tell her anything about me knowing about the end of Granddad. She is too elated. "That was amazing, what happened with Catty the other night," she says, stripping down and heading for the shower. "I wanted to tell you about it immediately, but I didn't want to wake you and I had to keep Mama from driving me crazy, so I went to New Orleans with her." She walks into the bathroom, leaving the door open. "Why did you leave the other night?"

"It's not really my thing, you know. I got scared, I guess. All complicated. Three people."

"You know what Catty said to me? She said, 'You know, I loved the way Boz let me touch his chest. I've never felt such a welcoming chest.'"

"She said that? I have a really small, bony chest."

"Well, she said that."

"Did she say anything about Kyle?"

When she walks back from the bathroom, she is naked and shiny, her freckles never more perfect. "I asked her if he was her lover and she said to me, 'Kyle is Kyle.'

Whatever that means. Boz, you know you were there with us, don't you? Just because you left, doesn't mean you weren't there. Catty said to tell you that you made her night."

I have the urge to hear Catty's voice again, so I replay her record as Meg gets in the tub.

"You hear that voice, that's what her body feels like, rough and soft and new, but like a real home," she says, splashing around in the tub. "Like you Boz, you are one of the most comfortable places in the world too."

I remember Catty's hand on my chest. "Are you going to be okay when they leave?" I ask.

"I don't think they're leaving," Meg says. "They say they are, but I don't believe it."

"How do you know?"

"Because," she says, "that would be like Elizabeth Taylor leaving Montgomery Clift at the bottom of the hill without pulling the teeth out of his throat. They just won't leave us like that."

As we listen to Catty's record, Meg returns to the tub, and is splashing around like a child. I worry for Meg. But mostly I worry for Granddad whose image I can see more clearly now. I can see him waiting for me to get up around six A.M., and going to discover him in his bed. He will have stopped breathing only a few moments earlier.

14

Granddad has to die to be forgiven. When I find him in his bed at 6:13 A.M. with the morning paper on his stomach, his hands folded across his chest, I know the town will lose their grudge.

When good people like Granddad die, all is forgiven. This is why the flowers have started filling the funeral home and the diner. People I haven't seen in ages, like Phyllis Jones, the woman who runs the local Christian bookstore, comes by to say how sorry she is. She is glad he didn't suffer. Everyone pretty much says, "I'm glad he didn't suffer." I want to point out that he did suffer, not from illness, but from them.

"What should I do?" Meg asks. "I've always hated everyone I knew who died. What do you do when you don't hate someone who dies?"

"You don't hurt yourself," I say. "That's what you do, you don't hurt yourself. Nothing. That's what you do. You don't have to do anything at all."

When I had gone into the old house earlier this morning, I wasn't the least bit scared of what I'd find. I was assured by something last night of exactly what I'd discover. The cuckoo clocks were all going crazy by six thirty and the dust had grown even thicker.

I used to fantasize about how I could pay Granddad back for taking care of me all those years. I always wanted to get rich and buy him a better boat. Or drink less and not worry him so much when I stayed out late. Or that I would go to college, marry a nice girl, and settle down and have him come live with us in a two-story house. But the only thing I was ever able to do for Granddad was to be around. And I know that counts for something, but he gave me more than most people whose parents leave them ever get. Granddad is the reason I'm not in situations like Jose or G.

When you spend your entire life watching people die young, seeing someone live a long life seems like a miracle. So all I feel immediately about Granddad's dying is that there are conversations already missing from my life. But I still believe I should feel more pain, more sadness.

Meg goes with me to the funeral home where the smell of flowers and formaldehyde make us both nervous and scared, as if we have just died too.

"It'll hit you, Boz. You're just in shock." Everyone has a theory about grieving. We are sitting in one of those dark, expensive, library-looking rooms waiting for the funeral director to come talk to us.

"I'm not in shock," I say. "It's already hit me. Granddad's dead. I knew it before it happened."

"Boz, you sounding crazier than me."

I do feel a bit crazy and out of place. I still can't accept it completely. But it's as if Meg and I are precocious children playing out these adult roles in some twisted board game where the goal is to buy graveyard plots and bury people.

"Meg, let's just do it all tonight and in the morning, if we can. Granddad would have wanted it over quick. He would have said, 'There ain't no sense in making a big deal about it. There's no need for no foolishness.'"

"If that's what you want," she says.

"It's what he wants," I tell her.

People in Noxington haven't been dying much lately, so that allows arrangements are made quickly. It is going to be the wake of the man everyone has been so mad at for bailing G. out of jail.

"He had his stubborn ways, but was a good ol' soul," Mr. Locklin, the assistant D.A., says, passing us in front of the courthouse on our way home.

The diner is quiet and feels colder than ever because we crank up the air conditioner. This is something Granddad would never allow. "Meg, I don't really have anyone else but you."

"Neither do I," she reminds me. "Not really."

Funerals and wakes in Noxington are like sad garden parties. Some people almost keep a scorecard of how many they've been to. William McClain was notorious for attending wakes. He once showed up for the wake of a man who hadn't even died. Then when William himself died, hardly anyone showed.

I want this to be different, I want them to respect Granddad again, and I want it to be over. That's what Granddad would have wanted too.

Meg doesn't have any funeral clothes at my place, and I don't really have funeral clothes at all. I put on my black Sunday suit with its too-short sleeves and high pant legs. She is wearing a short black dress, her only one with sleeves. We are both thinking about missing Catty's performance tonight, but neither one of us wants to talk about it. Finally, I say, "Catty'll have a packed house. She won't even notice us not being there."

There are about fifty people at the wake, mostly crowded into the small kitchen, drinking coffee, talking about how much they will miss the diner if it doesn't re-open. "What's gonna happen to it now?" a woman I don't recognize, wearing a blonde wig and a green dress, asks me.

I ignore her and go to sit on one of the elegant sofas by myself. I am thinking about Granddad fishing in the lake, throwing back everything he caught because he never wanted to see the fish die.

By ten, everyone is gone. I haven't even looked at Granddad in the coffin, and I won't. I have seen him dead in the most real way, the only way dead people are really meant to be seen.

These people don't know that this morning, when I found him dead, as I had predicted, everything stopped for me. I had walked over to his bed. And that house, with all its crazy clocks and fans, was completely silent. I had walked over to him, and I rested my head on his chest. "Granddad," I told him, "Thank you. Thank you. Thank you." And then I had rested beside him for about twenty minutes and I talked to him. "What do you expect me to do now?" I'd asked him, crying and laughing and crying some more.

My heart is still broken, but Granddad taught me that it is possible to keep going on even when your heart stops beating.

15

When we get back to the diner, we see them standing outside. Kyle looks somber, as if he needs to crawl between someone's legs and be cradled. "I'm sorry," he says.

"It sure hurts to lose someone." Catty seems a little drunk, and she proves this by going on to say something about herself. "I lost the audience halfway through. It was horrible, the worst ever."

I unlock the diner and we go in, settling lazily into booths and on the tops of tables as if it were a living room. I can already hear Granddad's voice, starting, saying, "Let this old man tell you something..." Now I am missing him more.

"We're leaving first thing in the morning," Catty announces. "So we wanted to see the two of you."

I watch Meg go from pale pink to ghost white. Knowing her, I am sure that she wants to kick and scream, but she just stands still.

"This shit can really be upsettin'," Catty says. "Boz, are you going to be all right?" She asks this with a sober directness, like it is her grandfather who has just died.

"I've been through worse," I say, trying to let go.

Kyle jumps in. "I know, Boz. About the fire, about your mother."

"I'll be fine," I numbly tell them.

Then Catty walks over and rubs my shoulders, the way she's rubbed my chest all those days ago. "There's nothing much worse than losing somebody you love."

I don't want to tell or remind them that I know this, considering my family's connection to death. I look at them, and am not sure if I want them to know my secrets. After all, they can run away with them. When I don't answer, Catty jumps in.

"Okay, let me cheer y'all up. I was singing on that stage and just before I sang 'Baby, It's Us' some drunken asshole yelled out, 'Drop dead!' And I just stood there for a moment, thinking, wouldn't it be crazy if I just dropped dead right then and there. People will say anything, won't they?"

"Why are we talking about bad stuff tonight?" Meg wonders, sounding annoyed.

"Yeah, why?" Kyle asks.

"I thought it was funny. I guess it came out all wrong." Catty puts her arms around me and kisses me on the neck. Her breath feels so good. I start to get hard.

"When Catty gets drunk, she gets darkly humorous," Kyle informs us.

"I ain't drunk," she says. "Gettin' drunk, but not drunk. Yet."

"It's okay, Kyle," I say. "I like to talk about dark, bad stuff. Even when I'm not drinking."

Kyle rolls his eyes a bit. "See what you started, Catty?"

"Come to think of it," Meg says, resting on one of the tables and staring at the ceiling, "Boz does love dark memories."

"But maybe not tonight, Boz. I'm sorry love, I didn't want to upset you." Catty is still wrapped around me. "Do y'all want to go for a ride?" she asks. "Does anybody else want a drink?"

There is something about being in the diner with them that makes me feel everything is going to be okay.

"Tonight at the wake, everyone was wondering why I am not more upset. They made it sound like I didn't love Granddad or something. But that's not it at all," I say, sprawled in one of the booths. "A death like Granddad's is peaceful, compared to other stories in my family. But you'd never understand Granddad unless you knew those stories."

"Boz, baby, let's go tie one on. You don't have to get into all this stuff tonight," Meg says.

My head is full. Catty's voice plays over and over again, Kyle's fists hit the red bag, Meg's fingertips on my wrists at night. Even in silence, they captivate me.

"Where do you all want to go?" Meg asks.

"I say we leave it up to Boz," Kyle says.

But I'm not really listening to them. I don't want to go anywhere. I want to stay right here.

"Boz?" one of them asks.

There are moments when you realize that you may never again have a chance to tell certain stories. I am angry that Catty and Kyle are leaving tomorrow. And I know that no matter what I say, even if Meg's heard it before, she'll starve or cut herself over it.

I am now sitting on the floor, leaning against one of the booths, my hands wrapped around my legs. "My mother walked into our burning house when I was a kid," I begin. "Y'all know about that. My father was a lunatic. That's why she did it. I don't blame her. But they were both crazy. My sister went to live with an older cousin in New Orleans and I never heard from her again. I used to imagine how she turned out, a Garden District princess or a homeless junkie by the river. But with my Granddad working offshore at the time, it was a world with just him and me."

I don't look at them as I speak, instead I just keep going. "And I'd watch my dad drink clear alcohol from small, square bottles. But even when he was sober, he'd sit and watch me from the other end of the table while I did my homework. He drank that alcohol like it was life. Even when he was sober he always looked at me like he'd never seen me before. After my mother died, I'd just lay there under the pillows he'd try to smother me with, waiting, wanting to die the way I assume old sick men who've been suffering too long want it to end. But I always lived. Always."

Breathing is something I often have trouble with when talking about this stuff. "I longed for a belt. Got jealous when other kids at school told me about their spankings. Being whipped seemed the fancy way to be punished. I wanted to be beaten the way other kids were."

I lay on the floor, trying to breathe normal, wanting to go on.

"That's a horrible story, Boz." Catty's voice is almost a whisper.

"Boz, you don't need to do talk about this tonight..." Meg's still trying to stop me.

"Then, when I was twelve, there was a man hanging from the Ferris Wheel. It was October, near midnight, and I was playing that game where you put a quarter on a color and see which color hole the hamster runs into. The midway was about to close, with just a few people still left, including my dad who always worked one of the rides each year. I saw all these people looking towards the Ferris Wheel. I followed the crowd. And you could see them turning the wheel, bringing him down. I moved in closer and could see the noose was so tight around his neck that I was surprised they could even get it off. His eyes were open and I moved even closer, it seemed he was looking at me. He was Donald Davis, my dad's drinking buddy. He came over to the house to play cards a lot. I expected him to get up and start talking to me. I'd heard stories of this happening. But he didn't. He just lay there dead. I started looking for my father. Then I realized that I was free to spend the night wandering the fairgrounds, hiding from the cops and everyone else."

They are all listening intently now, sort of hovering together on one of the tables. Then there is quiet.

"I slept on the damp grass near the Zipper ride that night, thinking I'd leave when the carnival did, or ride away on one of the rodeo horses in a nearby stable."

I am all laid out now, feeling that cool diner floor like I am on the grassy fairground. I think if I look hard enough at the ceiling, I'll be able to see stars. "When one of your parents goes out in a crazy way, you're branded. When they both do it, you might as well be a circus freak."

I want to tell them more. "Nobody was looking for me at the fair. Certainly not my father. They had already taken him away, but I didn't know that. This wasn't the first time I'd been separated from him. Sometimes he would lose me at the A&P or the movie theatre. We had an unspoken rule that if that happened, I'd just walk home. My father and I lived privately. People hated him, so there was nobody else to really notice I was gone. Someone has to know you exist to know you're no longer there."

I am breathing slower now, still searching for at least one star on the ceiling. "I stayed at the fair for two days. Then Granddad came from offshore and some policemen came and got me and took me to his house. Granddad didn't give me all the details. But later on, I found out that they were fighting over a fifty dollar card game debt. He didn't know how angry my father was, and my father, who usually worked the Hurricane ride, was working the Ferris Wheel that year. At some point, just after the Ferris Wheel shut down, he strangled Donald and hung him on its spokes. He said in court that he knew he'd get caught. I never saw him again. He went to Angola for life, and then one night, he did to himself what he done to Donald. He hanged himself in his cell."

"Oh, sweetness," I hear Catty say.

"Granddad didn't promise me big things. He simply said, 'This old man ain't never had a boy. With your grandmamma gone, I don't know how to have a kid on my own.' I just let him talk to me the way I'd let my father talk to me, not saying a word. Then he said, 'Let this old man tell you something, I'll do my best.'"

The diner is still and quiet and I figure that they've either left or fallen asleep, but I go on. Stories like this can run people off. "I looked across the table and Granddad said, 'You'll be mine.' And that was the first time any man ever told me anything I believed."

There are still no stars on the ceiling, just me on the hard floor. I am crying. Not sobbing. I never cry that way, though I envy people who can. Instead, there are just tears rolling down my cheeks like when I was eight and got the Holy Ghost for the first time.

A sudden feeling of hunger sweeps over me. Now I can feel them around me, can feel them breathing, like waking up and knowing that you're not alone. I start to say, "See, it's no big deal. It's over." But before I can speak, they move in close like lights. Then they put their hands on me. All of them. Kyle holds each of my hands in his, Catty keeps rubbing my neck and Meg lies across my torso. It is so good to be touched, especially by people who I am sure have their own stories.

Catty gets up and puts the B-side to a Van Morrison song on the jukebox. Kyle's hands grow warmer. Meg clings tighter, as though she is attached. When Catty returns, she puts my head in her lap, gently stroking my hair as she hums along to the music.

They love me and touch my body in ways that I did not know I could be touched. They touch each other. And it is wonderful. Time has been stopped. I am in the diner, but I am a million miles away. We all are.

16

I must sleep well on that diner floor because not even the fiery bright morning sun wakes me. I am hungover from last night. As I look around, I don't see Meg anywhere. Beneath my head, someone has placed the black-and-white Led Zeppelin pillow I won years ago at the arcade. Someone has placed a sheet over me. I recognize the small red ink stains on it. It's the one that Kyle and I dried off with. I can smell him on its off-whiteness.

I stay disoriented. The blinding sun, the slow remembrance of the previous night's revelations, make me rise. I walk to the window in a drunken way and look outside. There are two passersby peering at me in my underwear, one of them pointing, one laughing uproariously. My attention shifts to what is no longer outside. The red car is gone. They are gone.

I go upstairs, half-naked and in a hurry, searching for Meg who isn't here either. I am the only person alive. And I punch myself in the right thigh, feel some relief, wishing I had the courage to punch myself in the gut with such force. I now understand why Meg cuts herself.

At first, I search the room for a sign of them: a note, a piece of clothing, a whiskey bottle. But during my pacing, my anger turns to sadness because I feel as though they have tricked me. I begin to tear the room apart, throw *Broken English* and *Baby, It's Us* across the room, tear down my Dwight Yoakam poster. Soon most of my records are scattered around the room along with my movie tapes.

Then, there it is. A note on the turntable written in blue ink on Catty's yellowing record sleeve. It is one of those notes not about the future. Catty has written: *If only we could stay and hold you forever, we would. Love, Catty.* Kyle has added, in the same ink but with much clearer and larger handwriting, *Sorry– Kyle.*

I throw a few more things around the room, my favorite thickest pillow, a small Rolling Stones tongue mirror. Some things get thrown for a second time. I want to kill them for leaving. I want to kill myself for letting them go. I could have begged them to stay, or asked to go with them. Now I understand Meg's wanting them to stay and how she has gone into her state of denial about them leaving. She is probably with them, though. I can picture the three of them driving away, the wind blowing against them at just the right speed, the future being whatever they want.

Meg is sobbing loudly as she enters the room. That's how she cries, and if you don't know any better you think she is laughing. But just like me, she isn't wiping the tears away.

"How could they leave us?" Being around Meg when she is hysterical makes me feel calm.

"We knew, Meg. They told us all along."

"Last night I thought I would get them to stay. I thought you would be able to." She throws herself across my bed with great force.

All day, we stay inside putting the room I've tried to destroy back together.

"Why didn't they love us like we needed them to?"

"Maybe they do," I assure her. "Catty's got her shows, her

career. Meg," I say, pulling her almost weightless body into my arms, "this is the only thing I know. People will leave you. And you will leave people. That's all I really know for sure."

Meg stays red for a week from crying. The doctor, who she sometimes says is saving her and other times says is trying to kill her, has put her on some new blue pills. They make her want to sleep all the time. At times, I want to go see that doctor myself. She wakes up, stumbles around, and eats a few pretzels or jellybeans before going back to bed. "This medication is supposed to work. The last one didn't." She says this, her speech all slurred. Her head seems to be growing bigger as her body grows smaller.

I try to focus on getting the diner back together. But I feel lost. And I can't help but worry that I am like my father. He mastered the art of sitting and staring long ago.

I try to get Meg out of this room by getting her to come to Granddad's with me. She tries but falls asleep as we cross the main road. A few truckers watch as I carry her skinny body back upstairs.

I end up going alone and find that Granddad has collected even more junk than I thought he had. There are a lot of books about World War II, the war he fought in. There are also many strange chests with nothing but cheap shirts that have never been taken out of their wrappers. In the dusty kitchen of all places, there is a chipped trunk with dry-rotted sheets and linens. There are cracked dishes, maybe antique, though I can't really tell the difference, in a box in the bathroom. There is an old toilet in the attic.

While it is all very cobwebbed and dusty, with pictures of

dead people on the wall, it isn't spooky. In fact, Granddad's ghost would be a welcome sight, his voice and face would not scare me at all.

Never trusting banks, I know that he's kept his personal money in a green, metal box in his locked bedroom closet. I think Granddad can see me kick in the door. He always told me where the money was.

Days long ago, finding fifty-thousand dollars in a green box would have set me free. It doesn't look like money is supposed to look when you see a lot of it at one time. Money-green instantly becomes the dullest color I have ever seen. The more I understand that there is nothing keeping me in Noxington now but me, the blurrier the green bills become. I can get on a bus. I can even take a plane.

I spend the next day with the lawyer. I've managed to find the original will in another box near the green one. It is no surprise that Granddad has left it all to me, consisting mostly of the contents of the house, the house itself, and the diner. I need all these things, especially the money. But I don't desire it the way I assume one desires a decent amount of money.

What I want are people. One who has fallen into an endless state of sleepiness in my bed, one who has fallen asleep forever, and the two who have flown away in a red car.

"Boz Matthews, your granddaddy would have wanted you to keep the diner open," John Brians, the man who had cut my hair since I was a child, tells me. His hands shake these days from Parkinson's, much worse than Kyle's nerve damage. He still gives the best cuts in town, even if at times it does seem like he might accidentally take an ear off.

"I haven't decided what I'm gonna do."

"This town misses your Granddaddy. He was one of the only honest ones. When I started this business on the GI Bill, he was one of my first customers and he said to me, 'You're gonna be here a long time.' I believed him. He was a good man." He is finished with the cut, and is dusting the back of my neck, using that certain talcum powder which reminds me of a time before I was even born. "So what you gonna do if you don't open the diner?"

"I have no idea," I say. "Maybe open a barbershop."

It always takes him a minute before chuckling. "If you think you good enough to compete with me, then go ahead." He slaps me on the back as I hand him a ten-dollar bill. "Your granddaddy, he'd talk about you and say how glad he was that you wasn't like everybody else."

John Brians can talk forever, so I walk out the door and he stands facing me from the doorway. "Boz," he says, a little more serious, a little quieter, "remember when your daddy got locked up and your granddaddy brought you in here, and your hair was so long I mistook you for a girl?"

I am still embarrassed about this.

"Most men woulda been ashamed, but he said, 'That grandson of mine ain't like nobody else in town.' Then he smiled. He liked that idea."

"I ain't like all the others in town?" I inquire.

"Well, we all have our peculiar ways." He says this as he steps back into the shop, allowing me to leave, probably before he tells me how he really feels about my peculiar ways.

Rumors have begun circulating about Granddad. About

how much money he had, some saying he was a millionaire who lived like a pauper. In reality, the house is only valued at ten thousand dollars, the diner at twenty thousand, two thousand dollars in the bank, and the fifty thousand in cash. They also start the rumor that one of his ex-convict employees killed him and ran off with his money.

Loneliness is making me agitated, making me restless, especially combined with the fact that I've confessed my most embarrassing secrets to almost-strangers on the diner floor. Or it might be the simple fact that I am tired of overhearing people talk about Granddad's money. I haven't watched *A Place in the Sun* for weeks or listened to *Tapestry* in just as long. I've stopped wondering where those trucks on the highway are headed.

17

He starts keeping me awake at night. Granddad does. I sometimes wake up sneezing to the scent of dust from the old house. Or I'll awaken and recognize the scent of English Leather cologne drifting through the room. And my sleep begins to be broken up by full conversations with him.

"Why do you pace the room? Walk the stairs?" I ask him one night, half-asleep, unable to see him, but sure of his presence.

"Why do you stay in bed?" he responds.

"Why not?"

"Why don't you re-open the diner?"

"Why don't you?"

"Because this old man dead."

"Me too," I say.

This is how we talk to one another in mid-sleep, in the afternoons, and also late at night. Anytime I think of the money or selling the diner, he comes to visit. I am in bed most of the time, only going out once in a while to get a beer from The Tavern or to buy groceries. When Meg and Catty and Kyle were around, I'd felt I could do anything. Now all I think about is leaving, even though I know I will get sick if I try to. So when I am not in the darkened diner or my room, I look at maps.

I want to go to places, not because of what it is supposed to be like there, but because of the way it is shaped on the map. For example, Italy fascinates me because it looks like this very state but is so far away. And Alaska because it's all by itself.

I know I can leave quickly, once the will is probated. I can even buy my own red car and let the wind hit me in the face. I have the cash now, but am almost afraid of it, afraid to spend it because I think Granddad won't approve, and he'll come to me at night and tell me so. I also don't want all that dizziness and nausea that comes with leaving this place.

For the first time since his passing, I really want Granddad to go away. To disappear from my world, especially at night. I want him to tell me to leave, to break free. But I'm not so lucky.

"Stay."

"But they hate me."

"You hate you."

"They hate me more."

"Fight."

"I'm not a fighter."

"Everyone is a fighter."

These conversations, which I wake up having with him, are making me think that maybe I belong in the type of place they've taken Meg to. Where it is a way of life to have conversations with the dead.

I have nothing holding me in Noxington but bad memories, exclusion, and death. It's funny how such unpleasant things make me feel safe and secure and ultimately unable to move. Only those who've ever been trapped somewhere understand what it's like to stay stuck.

Early Saturday morning, when I have nothing to do but dream, I get a call from Meg.

"I'm outta here, Boz. They have me so zombied up."

"Don't come here," I say. "Your daddy'll kill us both." After

I say this, I realize this might make her want to come more.

"I can't take it in here," she wails, then I hear someone fighting her for the phone, then the connection is lost. I begin to fantasize about the places they send Meg to. Maybe I can spend the fifty thousand dollars to join her in a psychiatric ward.

Feeling like a prisoner with an option to leave but with no idea of where to go, dreading the motion sickness of travel, I sleep with my maps. I hope this will help me decide which interestingly shaped place I might one day soon get the guts to run off to. No matter how old you are, when you've never left home, it always feels like you are planning to run away.

I like the idea of California, of those hills that James Dean sped down. But according to the two great biographies on him, he liked New York as well, maybe even more so. Certain ghosts like his still guide me, even more than the maps.

When dusk comes, I sit in the window and wait for that dreaminess I held not so long ago to return to me.

Instead, the dreams I now have are in my sleep and the night after Meg's phone call, a crazed Granddad comes to visit.

"Stay."

"No."

"Stay."

"I want to go."

"To where?"

"Wherever!"

"You're already there."

Not having slept well because of all this ghostliness, I am awakened by a loud, booming knock on my door around eight

A.M. It is a scary knock, the kind that policemen and mean drunks are so good at.

I stumble to the door barely dressed, shirtless in black underwear. It is Meg's mother. She is wearing a light blue pastel outfit. Her hat doesn't match today. She has, for some reason, chosen a yellow one. I know that the Pentecostal church does not approve of wearing hats.

"Good morning, Boz."

I let her in. What makes her so different is how much smaller her face looks. It seems less round, as though some of the anger she had just a couple weeks earlier has moved to her belly.

After having only spoken to the dead for the past week or so, I don't know what to say to her or to anyone for that matter.

I look around my place, which is a mess. "Why don't we go downstairs to the diner?" We don't talk on the way down the stairs, and, entering the diner, I am a little dazed, but not fearful of her. We sit at one of the booths where my recently departed friends once sprawled.

I haven't raised any of the blinds in the diner, and feel that the darkness suits us. "How is she?"

"She's okay. But she told me everything."

"Everything about what?"

"About you and her and the baby."

"What?" My elbow slips and the wobbly table shakes. I wonder if this is the insanity Granddad wants me to stick around for.

"She's two months along. She wants to keep it. I know I have been angry with you many times, but Boz, it is your baby and Meg wants to be with you." She keeps making the table wobble, too, obviously as nervous as I am. "Boz, I know this is a small-minded town. Preacher Richards and I were talking. If the two of you want to be together, all right. But maybe a bigger city is better, like New Orleans or Houston."

"She's two months pregnant?" I ask.

"Yeah. She loves you Boz. How do you feel about moving away with her and the baby? The new Pentecostal church he's started won't accept this."

I am stunned at Meg's slick ability to tell such a story. I don't want any part of this.

"I can't leave Noxington. Not yet. There's legal stuff to be settled."

"How about after that?"

"I'll think about it."

"We'll give y'all money," she says.

"Let her come back here and let's see how we get along. This is some crazy shit," I say.

She looks at me with suspicion, squinting, like I am bringing her shocking news by not falling for her powerful smile. Her face starts to become bloated, just like I've seen it be many times before. It is the look that people who have nothing but money on their side get when they realize even that might not be enough.

Instead of exploding, she sighs and says, "Boz, okay. I'll let you two try it. But don't do any of that crazy stuff that gets everybody talking."

"What crazy stuff?" I ask.

"Drinking. Walking all over town at odd hours. Hanging

out with degenerates like Kyle Thomas and that unrespectable, weird lady friend of his. By the way, you'll have to get married at some point. Just something quiet, keep all this quiet, okay?"

"Where is she now?"

"She'll be coming in on the bus from New Orleans tomorrow. She didn't want us to pick her up."

"Mrs. Richards, why did you change your mind?"

"My daughter is mentally unstable. But I figure she ought to be allowed to be around people that she loves."

She gets up and grips me tight, holding me in that way that hurts but is supposed to make a person feel good. "Boz, you have a good soul. I know you've got some ways like a hooligan, but you do have a soul. It's a shame that you have to be so different." She starts towards the door, catches a glimpse of herself in the rusted mirror next to it. "If she starts going off the deep end, let us know." She is still staring at herself.

"Are you all right?" I ask.

She simply shrugs and exhales heavily through her nose, as one of those unreadable smiles comes across her face. "My goodness," she says. "I put on the wrong hat this morning. I can't believe it. I guess I'll have to go back home and change. They say hats are of the devil. Maybe they are right."

The very next day is one of the first non-blisteringly hot days since summer began. I meet Meg at the bus stop across the street from the old post office. She gets off carrying nothing but a small, navy duffel bag and is wearing one of those big hats that cover a person's entire head, hiding herself.

"You look great, Meg," I say, pulling her close, her bones moving likes snakes through her body. She still hasn't been eating properly, but she is as wide-eyed as I have ever seen her.

"I'm beat," she says. "Buses, even for the shortest distance, wear me out." Then she reaches up, gently touches the left side of my face. "Boz, knowing that you were here, out here, is all that kept me going. You've got something that makes people not be able to stay away from you."

I don't know what to say.

"It's a good thing, Boz. It's magic."

"Meg," I say, taking her bag, walking through the dusty air. "People leave me. That's the gift I have, the gift of running people off."

"The people that ran away from you are people who didn't know you well enough," she says.

"Jesus, what kind of fucking drugs do they have you on?"

"I'm not on anything," she says. "For the first time in years. Except for a little pot."

We are quiet as we near the diner. I don't want to mention her lie about the pregnancy just yet. I'll wait until we get upstairs. Her bag is light. Even carrying nothing would weigh her down.

As we climb those stairs, which I know will fall soon if I don't get someone to fix them, she says, "I can't stay away from you. I've tried and I can't."

"So what happens when your father finds out you're lying?" I ask her.

"About what?"

"The baby." I say. "The one you told your mother about so you could come back here."

"Boz, I didn't create the baby. We did."

"Meg! This is serious. Get a fucking grip!" I stand and walk over to her. "I never fucked you. We've done other stuff. But Meg, we didn't do anything to make a baby and you know that." I suddenly don't want her around.

"It's not just yours and mine. All of ours. That night?"

"That night?"

She points to the bed and I sit down beside her, my head hanging. She puts her hand on my arm, but I shake it away. "That night when you cried yourself to sleep on the floor of the diner. After that, Catty just laid there, touching herself, layin' her head on your chest, touching herself as she watched Kyle and me do something more. That's what happened, but Boz, it wasn't just Kyle and me, it was all of us. All of us created this life inside of me."

I feel myself growing dizzy with emotions that make me ache. I have never felt so betrayed in my life. "So you managed to get both of them? Am I that fucking weird and ugly that I can't be touched? I'm the sleeper of the group, I guess." I get up and walk to the window and back, want to cry because she's had both of them. "It sounds like Kyle is the one you ought to be talking to."

"Boz," she says softly, but I ignore her.

"Listen," I say, back at the bed, I don't want anything to do with it. I give up my fourth of a right to the baby. I don't even claim an arm or a leg or an eyelash. No. And how dare you put this baby on me! What gives you the right to say it's my baby?" I kick her bag across the room.

"Because, that night," she says as calmly as if I weren't in a rage, "you laid there on the floor and you seduced us all."

"Well, I didn't fucking mean to."

"Boz, I'm telling you." She is sitting up now, clutching a pillow. "Something was in the room that night. The way you were laid out on the floor like you'd just spoken in tongues. You looked like one of those toppled religious statues that cries real tears. So that's why." She places her hands on her stomach. "This baby is yours, too."

"What does that mean?" I am sitting at the window again. "How do you assign a baby like that? It's not right."

"What happened that night was beyond any of our control."

"Maybe you should go be with your Jesus parents or go back to the hospital. I thought you were well thirty minutes ago, now I realize you're more on the edge than ever."

She storms out of the room, and I later find her sitting on the stairs, picking at the chipped wood. "Meg, I'm sorry. It's just that this is a lot. You can stay as long as you want as long as we pretend the baby doesn't exist, at least for a couple of days."

"No problem," she says. "I pretend it doesn't exist almost all the time anyways. I'm good at that."

18

But there is going to be a baby. In the night, when the ghosts of past visitors and certain tormented actors come, I place my hand on her stomach and think of Catty and Kyle. At times, it is as if they are lying in bed with us. I am still angry that they left us, but it doesn't feel they are truly gone when I touch Meg's beautiful belly in the moonlit room.

Granddad doesn't visit as much anymore and I miss those conversations I'd started to hate. Instead, I am haunted by those still living. People like Catty, Kyle, and everyone else who ever walked out on me. I don't tell Meg that I touch and feel her wonderful belly in the night while she sleeps like a baby herself.

Our lives go on. Meg wakes up early in the morning and pukes and goes for walks. This is a healthy sight to see from someone like her. She is only taking some vitamins now. I know she needs a regular doctor, but I know that mentioning it will force her to accept what has happened between her and Kyle. I know that eventually her father and mother will come and check up on us, but for now we continue to deny parts of this new life.

One morning, when she is supposed to be out for her walk, I hear her yelling from the window down below. "Boz, I need help!"

She looks like a summer bird that can soar gloriously into the air. But this time she is firmly grounded, with the shock and panic only in her eyes. "Get down here."

When I reach the bottom of the stairs, I turn the corner. Near the bathroom door is Catty Mills, passed out on the ground. I gently lift her up and drag her slowly into the diner.

Catty is breathing and muttering something about ice cream and blue water. She smells like The Tavern at the end of a night. She is wearing one of her short dresses, which is twisted and pulled in all directions. Meg grabs a pillow and an afghan from upstairs. "Is she gonna die?" Meg asks.

"No. This is not death."

Catty's dress is pulled down in the front, open, revealing her scar. In the light of the diner, it looks like an arrow pointing somewhere, in some direction, like if we look at it long enough it will tell us exactly what to do.

Her eyes open and close. I check her purse and find a bottle of yellow Valium filled just two days ago. There were sixty in the bottle and now there are only two.

"Catty, wake up!" I yell at her. "She needs to sit up to puke. Get me a trash can from the kitchen."

Meg acts swiftly, and I am grateful that she is in fairly good shape right now. I wouldn't be able to handle the two of them like this at once. Meg stands around, like a nurse, waiting for me to instruct her, she makes me feel like a doctor of sorts when it comes to these cases of people who verge between suicide and life. I lean Catty's head forward and she begins to throw up, getting some of what is inside of her and about to kill her out.

"She just needs to get rid of all that," I tell Meg.

"I can't watch," Meg says, but never stops looking. She is mesmerized by someone who is, in this moment, very similar. I see Meg see herself. Maybe after seeing this, she'll never try to kill herself with pills.

Catty is in the same place where I laid that night of my revelations. I am still holding her head up as she begins to open her eyes a little wider. Seeing them open the slightest bit, makes me sigh with a little relief.

As we bathe her, making sure she doesn't drown in my old tub, she begins to open her eyes slowly, briefly, then takes her fingers and blindly runs them along our faces. "Sweethearts," she whispers. As her eyes open more frequently, more quickly, she touches us more. Though she is becoming more familiar with her surroundings, she is still limp enough to be considered nearly gone.

When she is clean, we wrap her in a sheet and put her to bed. It has been a while since I've seen anyone broken down like this. Even Meg's attempts at dramatic endings haven't been this close to the edge of life or death or whatever it is people like them are searching for.

"How can you be sure that she won't die?" Meg asks, tugging at my right arm.

"Because I know," I say. "I just know."

"How?"

"I just do." And that is the real truth, I just know Catty isn't going away in the same way that I knew my grandfather was. "Trust me," I say, pulling Meg close to me. "I can tell."

"I can't watch this all night," she says.

"Maybe you should. You've looked like this so many times."

"That is why I can't watch."

Meg slams the door behind her. While she is gone, I walk

over and sit beside Catty.

I reach out and with my right forefinger touch her scar from the top and make my way down to the bottom of it. I'm drawn to the life that has been cut away.

As I continue to stroke her scar, her shivering stops and her skin seems to finally stop crawling.

Meg returns with an old pitcher from downstairs. She fills it with warm water and dips a washcloth. She begins to press the warm, torn yellow cloth against Catty's skin. I stop touching her scar, not wanting Meg to see me doing it. Touching it has definitely helped.

We don't sleep. We stay up, making sure she throws up when she feels the urge, and we turn the fan to her as she lies sweating. When she seems agitated, we talk to her, saying things that you say to people who could have just died. Things like, "Catty, remember that time you sang at the Opry?" or "Remember when you and Kyle picked me up in the rain?" Then, "Sleep. Just let go and sleep."

At one point, we turn on her record and let it fill the room. She is wide awake at this point, and she doesn't smile or say anything or seem any more energetic. But her eyes stay open, even if they don't see anything but the peeling bathroom door.

Meg and I have been so transfixed on her that we put on *La Dolce Vita* to distract ourselves. But Catty has the ability to pull us away from the movie with just a slight sigh or a rustling of the sheets.

At around five A.M., during the part where Mastroianni is introduced, she speaks. "I knew I could come here." Her speech is slurred, but understandable.

"Why here?"

"I had to come back to see you," she says, sits up, and goes right back down. "Come here," she says.

Meg looks at me, then immediately lies beside her. She strokes Catty's hair and they both look content.

"Boz, where are you Boz?" Catty asks. "Come hold me."

"Not tonight, Catty," I say from the foot of the bed as she reaches for me. "You need to rest."

Meg gives me a look of disapproval, as she wants me in bed too.

Just a couple of months before, the thought of jerking off with other people besides ghosts in the room would have been unimaginable. But I curl up, and, near the computer screen which is paused to Mastroianni at a party scene, I come.

I wonder if they see me, sort of not caring and sort of wanting them to.

19

Catty comes slowly back to life, but very quickly becomes more difficult, as she seems to think she is in some fancy hotel. She throws money at us and asks us to go get strange pesto and wheatgrass juice. These are things we've never heard of and things most of Noxington has not heard of either. "See if they have it somewhere," she says. Meg gets on the phone with her mother asking if she's heard of these products. She never has, but has a story about them anyways. "I think your daddy ate pesto once with the Deacons at that Italian restaurant on Dumaine. He didn't much care for it, but you know how hard he is to please. Wheatgrass? That's herbal stuff. You gotta be careful with that. You know, I have heard people get addicted to that, Meg."

Catty stays in bed for two weeks. We try to pacify her because we love her and want the vibrant Catty back. Besides, a demanding difficult Catty is better than no Catty at all. Because she has chosen my place out of all the places in the world to come to, I assume this means she maybe feels something towards me.

When I remind Meg that it's time for her go to her doctor, she shrugs, completely annoyed that now I am suddenly telling her to care about what is inside of her, who is inside of her. But she pauses and I can hear her swallow hard as she places her hand where I used to place mine in the night. She is still, as though she has lost the ability to feel. Then she says, "I can feel it. It's there. The baby inside of me.

Small, but it's there," she says.

She takes my hand and places her hand over her belly. She kisses me on the cheek. "I think I'll hitchhike to the hospital. I hate the emergency room and hospitals, but I think I'll go."

"I can come with you."

"Stay with Catty. She needs you now, too."

"I'll take care of both of you," I assure her.

Upstairs, Catty is expecting her. "Where's Meg?"

"She had to go someplace."

"Someplace where?"

"It's a secret. You'll find out."

"I love secrets!" she squeals. "Once when I was performing in Vegas, all the big shots at the time—Buck Owens, Roy Clark, two biggies—threw a surprise party for me. They kept it a secret for nearly a week."

I am sitting on the floor, flipping through the pages of a Rand McNally book, doing the map thing again. Sometimes I go online to see these places. "Boz, do you think I could just have a bit of whiskey?"

"No," I say.

"I think I might need it. It might make me feel better."

"No," I say again, noticing how Texas is so big that it makes Louisiana look like a mere attachment.

"Why don't you love me anymore?" She stops me dead, stops me from page flipping. "Every night I want you in this bed with us and still you refuse. Don't you remember?"

"Catty, I can't do it."

"Do what, honey? Come sit by me." Even though she says she isn't yet ready or able to get out of bed, she looks polished now. She is radiant again. But I know she isn't going anywhere just yet, if for no other reason, because there is no car for her to travel in.

"Two things," I say, standing. "You're well. You need to get out of that bed. I've had aunts that spent the last twenty years of their lives lying in beds or on sofas. Nervous southern women are prone to that."

"That's a fucking cliché," she says angrily.

"Well, it's what I've seen and you are too alive and too well for that."

She pauses for a moment, then looks away, pulls out a compact and looks at herself, looking like she doesn't even recognize her own reflection. "I know," she says. "I have relatives like that too. But I just need a couple more days."

"And the second thing is that I can't be the one loved less, the one that's only touched a little."

I walk over and put on some old Randy Travis. Catty shows some strength by getting up and literally pulls me down onto the bed. We end up lying there on our sides, staring at each other, face-to-face, totally safe in this position. "Boz, there are certain people so tender that you don't want to crush them or take advantage of them."

"We're all tender."

"But Boz, that night when you were on the floor of the diner and told your story, we wanted to protect you."

"Maybe I wanted more. . ." I say.

"None of us wants to hurt you, Boz."

She blinks slowly as we continue to lie, eye to eye, on our sides. "Boz, in all my years of brokenness and being drawn to brokenness, I'd never seen anyone tell a story of not falling apart the way you did that night. You got a power over people, Boz, but nobody wants to take a chance on hurting someone like you."

"I can't be loved, not when I tell that truth. I shoulda never told y'all."

"We love you all the way. We just feel protective."

"Remember," I say angrily, "this is the guy who dragged your ass up the stairs and saved your fucking life. What's weak about that?"

"Nothing," she says.

"I guess maybe we take turns being the child," I say, as she wraps her arms around my torso. "That night, you were the most loved person in the room."

"Then why did Kyle fuck Meg?"

"Because she's not broken in the same way. You can't tell Meg to eat, or mention her weight, but you can fuck her 'til she screams." She is stroking my hair. "You don't want girls, do you?"

"Not in that way. I used to. But I like to touch them and taste them and be touched by them. I want them to want me."

"I want you, Boz. Meg wants you."

"What about Kyle?"

"Kyle is Kyle. Don't try to figure him out."

"You know," I say, turning back to face her, "when you slept, I touched your scar. It was amazing. I rubbed it until you fell asleep."

"People are usually scared of it."

"I think it's the loveliest thing about you."

We kiss for a moment, and it feels perfectly romantic. We are tired. "Meg won't be back until tomorrow. And I have to tell you something. You've got to stop this demanding behavior. This isn't Hollywood. Or Nashville."

"I know I get a little carried away after I have a breakdown."

"I mean, we just don't want to spend all day looking for pine nuts and mascara."

"Boz, let me hold you tonight. I'll show you that I love you. We don't have to have sex."

"Well, I figured that."

"Why? Do you want to do that? Have sex?"

"No," I say as I pull off my white T-shirt and let her run her long nails along my thin chest until I fall asleep. But when I wake up a couple of hours later, I find my hardness pressing against her. She reaches out and touches it. When her mouth is on it, I let every worry go. "Catty," I say, pushing her back on the bed. "I want to. . . but I'm not sure I remember how. . ."

"I know," she says. This is the night I really learn how to use my tongue. She lets me find my way, lets me explore, lets me kiss her in that place that I've never wanted to kiss any woman before. It feels right, as she lets out a cry and shivers. As I rise, stroking myself, I let it out, all over her breast, her scar, her face.

As we lie there, falling asleep, she runs her fingers across my chest. "Catty, remember when you said that you didn't see any trash in here when you first arrived?"

"Yes, honey."

"Well, after knowing what you know about me and my family, do you think I'm that? You won't hurt my feelings. A lot of people think that about me."

"Think what about you?"

"That I'm white trash."

"No, honey," she says, her fingernails and Randy Travis lulling me to sleep. "You're not white trash. You're just grit, my love."

20

It is around three A.M., and the moon comes in brightly, just enough to give some light to lovers. Catty is telling us how she and Kyle split up this time. "We were in Biloxi," Catty begins. "I was supposed to be singing at the Riverboat Casino. And I had been drinking hot tea and bourbon all day. It usually helps my voice. Kyle got mad at me because I was having trouble getting it together for the show. I got a little too messed up. So driving along the beach in Waveland, he told me to get out of the car. So I did. I got out and began to walk along the beach, hitting every bar in sight, thinking Kyle would come looking for me. I slept on the beach and when I woke up, I took the Greyhound with the bottle of Jack and ate pills and drank all the way here. I was feeling like my life had ended somewhere onstage at that casino or on the beach."

Meg and I are listening closely, carefully taking it all in.

"Where is home to y'all?"

"New Orleans, but right now he might be at the little house on the water we have in Mandeville."

I take my cell phone outside to the spot behind the diner where I get decent reception. It is the middle of the night and I run my fingers over the phone, wondering if I should wait until the morning to call.

"Hello," he answers in his gentle, deep voice.

"Kyle, it's Boz. Boz Matthews. Are you all right?"

"Catty's there," he states bluntly.

"Yeah. But are you okay? Will you come to Noxington?"

"I don't think it's a good idea. She's gonna make me sad and angry without even meaning to. Sometimes we get like this. Sometimes we can't stand each other."

"I don't want to talk about Catty," I say. "I want to invite you here. It's not much of a place, I know. But I want to see you."

"Why do you want me back there?"

"Because I want to hear you hit your weight bag again, and hear the stories you still haven't told."

"Why do you care about those things?"

"I don't know, I just do. And after that night in the diner, your hands are on my mind. If you could just send your hands, maybe that would be enough, but you can't so can you please come see me in my rundown apartment. Just so I can see the hands that put my past to rest."

All I can hear are the cicadas and frogs, and I think he has hung up, then he says, "I'll try to make it. Good night."

"See!" Catty exclaims when I get back upstairs. "I know he still loves me. I knew he'd come for me." I let her think this, knowing it doesn't matter why he is coming, just that he is.

Meg looks upset. "Don't worry, Meg, it's all going to work out," I say, holding her close.

The more complicated that all of this gets, the more I am beginning to trust and believe them. Beginning to think that I can somehow control our destinies, plot our futures, create a place where we all end up with exactly what we want. I won't know it until later, but nobody has that kind of power. Especially not complicated lovers like us. And especially not people who have scars more alive than the rest of their bodies.

21

On a stroll along the highway, near Granddad's old house, I ask Meg if she knows any more about Catty's condition. "Is she really sick? Dying even?" I ask. "Cancer?"

"She told me she's fine, just can't physically get out of bed. I know what that's like," Meg says.

I pick up an old can in remembrance of Granddad and carry it, not sure if I'll ever let it go.

"She looks good," I say. "Rosy cheeks and glistening eyes and everything."

"And her voice is like it was before," Meg adds. She is right, Catty's voice once again sounds like it can either crack the television screen or melt the walls of the apartment.

We can hear Catty and Kyle yelling as soon as we return to the diner. His voice is overshadowed by the strength of hers. Meg and I sit on the steps, unclear of exactly what they are saying, not particularly wanting to know. Catty comes storming out of the house, mascara running, her voice deep and sobbing.

"Well you say you needed him here in order to get out of bed. So it worked," I tell her.

"Fuck you, Boz. That's not funny," she says, stopping in the middle of the stairs to put on her high-heeled shoes. "He told me he didn't come to see me. He came to see the two of you. Have him. I'm leaving. I can't be here now."

"Where are you going, Catty?" I ask.

"The motel or I'll sleep in the diner. I just can't be in that bed any longer. I think maybe you all want me to just disappear!"

She rages off in her best clothes, and we go upstairs, wondering what kind of shape Kyle is in. I wonder if we'll find him crying or with his fist through a wall. It is that mix of gentleness and violence that draws me to the room. Meg lingers behind and stands in the doorway, waiting for me to go find whatever there is to be discovered.

I go further in and then I see him through the bathroom door. And it is a beautiful thing to see. He is still fully dressed, in khakis and a light pink T-shirt, his dark hair curlier because of the steam from the hot water running full blast. He looks as though he does this all the time, as though taking baths fully clothed is the normal way to bathe. "I'm not going in there," Meg says under her breath.

"Maybe you should go lay down," I tell her. She does, though I can see her watching us through the open door. When I walk in, he seems a little spaced out, in an anger-induced trance. He doesn't seem annoyed that I just barged right in. "I made it. I came," he says sadly. "But it ain't right to fight like this in your place."

I sit on the side of the tub. "Look at how crazy she makes me. I'm sitting in a bathtub, fully clothed, soaking wet."

"Hey," I say, "whatever it takes to get you through the moment." He is still looking down, embarrassed. "God knows I've done some crazy shit." I am more entranced by his crooked nose, his muscles, and black curly hair than I was before. I am awed by the fact that he looks exactly the opposite of me: fair-skinned, blonde hair, skinny. I don't care if he sees me looking at him. He owes me at least this much.

"Catty makes us all mad," I say, "but she can't be all bad because she brought all of us together."

"Naw, she's not all bad. But I came to see you and Meg. Really." He looks at me when he says this, and some of the embarrassment seems to leave him. He grabs my wrist and just looks at me, squeezes tightly, then lets go.

"Why did you agree to come?"

"I told you. I wanted to see you. That night in the diner I learned that I could believe anything you say."

"I wanted to see you too," I say.

"Where is Meg?" he asks.

"She's in there. She can't handle people yelling and fighting. She'll calm down. Layin' in bed is her way of doing it." I look towards the bedroom and see her watching us. "She's looking at us right now."

He gives her a slight wave, and I'm sure telling him about the baby must be on her mind because she doesn't wave back, she just stares blankly at us. "Is this how you usually calm down? Fully clothed in a tub of water?" I ask him.

"No. Usually I take my clothes off first. Or I punch a bag. There's no bag here."

"Hit me," I say.

"What?" He laughs really loud, dismissing the seriousness of my offer.

"Hit me. I want to be your punching bag. I can take it. Just hit me. Anywhere."

He reaches out with both fists and comes at me. I can already taste the blood. Instead he keeps his fists tightly closed and wraps his arms around me. "People like you, I'd never punch." He is still holding me close. "You're like me, you've been punched enough. One more could kill you."

He lets go, having touched me, having hugged me the way a man does only when he means it, and not exactly sure how to let go. I stare at his soaking wet clothes.

"Well, you'll dry off. At least, you didn't hurt yourself the way Catty and Meg do."

"I don't understand that suicide thing," he says. "I don't know why they want to die or come so close to dying so often." He rests both arms on the sides of the tub. "Have you ever tried to kill yourself?"

I shake my head. "No. Since I had so many people around me die, there was never a reason to try to kill myself. At times, we're all already sort of dead."

"Are you going to stay in this town forever?" he asks.

"No. But I don't know where I'm going or what I'll do when I get there. Are you going to stay in that tub forever? Meg is out there, waiting to see you, too. She gets a little anxious about seeing people she hasn't seen in a while."

Meg is nervously sitting on the window ledge. The scars on her legs, the most obvious thing about her, make her look like a beautiful carving board. But she doesn't care. In fact, I think she is proud of them and enjoys showing them off.

She can't even look at Kyle who is undressing and drying off. "Meg, I came all this way to see you."

She still looks away. Wrapped in a blue towel, he walks over to her and sits beside her in the window. And to my surprise, I am not very jealous. In fact, I want to see them embrace, to see them touch. "What's wrong?" he asks.

Looking up at him, she says, "I never thought we'd see you again, then I thought you were just coming back to rescue Catty, then leave. Now I'm just really happy to see you." She reaches out for him and he embraces her in the same way he embraced me.

"I'm glad to see you two," he says, looking at me, then at her, then at me again.

"You guys wanna go for a ride, go out and get something to eat?"

For this moment, for the first time, we both have Kyle.

22

The navy-blue night embraces us as we grab some greasy cheeseburgers and devour them in the car, gorging ourselves like we are at Galatoire's. Meg is extremely happy to watch us eat.

Flying through the windy night is amazing, and for this moment, I stop wanting to leave. I am okay being here. I feel I can live the rest of my life like this. This would be even truer if Catty would come to her senses and return to us. I can't stop thinking about her scar and how much I miss it.

When we return, it is nearly midnight. I feel fine until we get into the apartment because wondering where everyone is going to sleep makes me nervous. It is not so much a feeling of jealousy this time, but more of a feeling of being a confused host.

Meg pulls her dress off and throws it across the bed. She's made her decision. "It's a big bed," I say to Kyle. "You two can fit there."

"And you?"

"I've got this sleeping bag."

"Are you sure?"

"Oh, yeah, I'm sure," I say, not actually sure at all.

He strips down to his plaid boxers and T-shirt, becoming an image out of a perfectly fucked-up underwear advertisement. I just curl into myself in the sleeping bag, which I place by the window.

There are some ghosts this night, only this time I don't

recognize them. I can hear them sleeping and breathing.

But at some point, probably around two A.M., Meg wakes up and says, "I need Boz in here too."

Kyle sits up. "I can take the sleeping bag."

"No," Meg says, "there's room for all of us. Let's just all lay together tonight. I really need that."

Kyle doesn't say anything else, he just falls back against the pillows, as Meg waits for me to crawl into the bed in between the two of them. She clutches my arm as my leg touches Kyle's. He doesn't move away from me, and soon I am being held by both of them.

We are all asleep when Catty opens the door. The other two keep sleeping when I sit up and stare at her. She is standing there in that way which makes it difficult to tell if a person is coming or going. But I know she's returning.

I stare at her for a while, and finally hold out my hand. I am just so glad to see her, but I also want to have this image of her in the doorway for as long as I can. "Come," I finally say. "Come to bed."

She kicks off her shoes and her everything else. Then she crawls against the wall, next to Meg. "I'm glad you're back," I say at one point, but she is already as asleep as the other two.

Everyone seems to sleep well. When I awake, it is early, around seven. Someone is missing from the bed. I check to make sure that everyone is still in the room. They are, but Kyle is awake and sitting on the torn, rough, gray carpet near the window.

"Did you sleep okay?" he asks.

"If I get five hours, I consider myself lucky," I say.

"I sleep an hour, wake an hour, sleep another hour, always have," he tells me. My brain doesn't let me pass out no matter how tired I am. I used to write songs like that. Now I just don't sleep well, and I don't write songs." He is shirtless and I have to tell him what I saw last night between the time Catty fell asleep and I dozed off.

"Kyle, last night while you were sleeping, I saw your scar glowing in the dark."

He laughs. "Boz, scars don't glow in the dark."

"Yours does. I watched it. It lit up the room. At first I thought it was the reflection from the bathroom mirror or the streetlight, or the moonlight, but it wasn't. It was your scar. Glowing."

"Boz," he repeats, pointing to the scar on the lower left side of his belly, "they don't glow in the dark. It's just a scar."

"Where did you get it?"

"When I was sixteen, I got in a fight with some dudes tougher than me." He is gazing down at it. "Boz, what did it look like?"

"Well," I say, touching it, tracing the whitish-pink outline of it with my fingertips. "At first it looked like Texas, then Italy, then California. It looked like every place I've never been. And in the end," I say, still touching it, "it looked like every place I have ever wanted to go."

He looks at me, seeming now to believe what I have seen. "You have been to all those places, haven't you?"

"Yeah, I have." He lies back and lets me touch it some more.

"It kept changing," I say.

"What does it look like now?"

"It looks like I can see the whole world on your belly. And when I touch it in just the right way, I feel like I've been there, too."

"Boz, nobody's ever noticed that scar so much. Not even Catty. I love hers, but mine bothers her."

"Well, it is there. The whole world on your lower left side."

"People always think it's a boxing scar. Isn't that crazy? Everyone knows people don't box with knives. They think boxers just go around fighting outside the ring, I guess. I thought about trying to have it covered at one point, but then I figured it didn't matter."

I am still touching it, mesmerized by its oddly changing shapes. Unlike Catty's scar, Kyle's isn't giving any direction, just showing what already exists in the world. "No. Keep it just the way it is. It's beautiful," I tell him. "So beautiful."

I reach down and stick my tongue out, touching him with it, tasting his sweat, and then I kiss the scar for a moment. He doesn't flinch. I rise, satisfied, and look at him.

"I'm glad you like it, Boz. But still, scars don't glow in the dark."

He lies there and doesn't seem the least bit uncomfortable by what has taken place. In fact, he seems more relaxed now. He stares at me like he believes me and likes this.

"Boz?"

"Yeah?" I ask.

"Touch it one more time. Do what you just did again."

I spend the whole next hour seeing the world.

23

As far as sex goes, there isn't much. But Kyle and Catty have forgiven each other by simply sharing my bed, which is just big enough for the four of us.

Right now, small adventures are all we need.

One of our favorite places to go at night is up near the old Kaiya Bridge. I know that quite a few people, at least a dozen, have died here, either by getting caught in the currents or by diving into a shallow area. But we don't go there for the water.

We go to that area to climb up the rusty back rail of one of the only billboards leading into town. Twenty years ago, this billboard advertised the motel. As a child, I always viewed it as a sad imitation of those motels advertised on game shows. It is the only motel in town, so I guess they don't feel the need to keep advertising here. And nobody else wants to use the space, saying it's too expensive, and that they'd rather advertise closer to town or online. It is as though Noxington is for Noxington people, and everybody who needs to know what is here, already does.

Now it is just a big empty board, a canvas for the imagination, informing travelers of the nothingness that exists ahead. But there is something about its partially cracked whiteness, about its faded cotton candy colors, that is inviting to people like us.

On this evening, we climb it like we always do, like it is a mountain that matters. Knowing we can go to jail for being up here makes it more exciting, makes us feel young again.

"I ain't climbing up there," Meg says. She has always been afraid to climb even before the pregnancy, a condition Catty and Kyle are still oblivious to.

Instead, Meg stays down below, turns on the car radio, puts on one of the CDs from Kyle's collection, blasts some rebelliously adult John Coltrane, and up on the ledge of that billboard on these summer nights, we look down on the town that is so much like other towns that we don't care to be part of.

Sometimes we dance along the billboard ledge and Meg moves gracefully on the ground below. Dancing up here is dangerous, but like drag-racing teenagers, we feel invincible. Perhaps this is why Meg bravely makes her way up for the first time.

So on this particular night, as Lou Reed sings about dark, dangerous streets in cities far away, we relax up high. I lay my head on Catty's legs and stretch out on the narrow ledge. I look at the full moon and this night I do see stars. When a town is asleep and you're this high up, the sky becomes your own.

Kyle is a little drunk, which is rare for him, rare for any of us except Catty. But even she hasn't been drinking in the past few weeks. She swears to have quit. "I am clean now," she says. "For good. The last thing I want is another rehab, and that's where I almost wound up this time. No. I feel good. No poison for me ever again." I know that she is still taking some Valium, but I don't say anything. I'm not sure that she thinks that counts. I'm not sure if it does or not.

Kyle's slight intoxication allows him to dance, not completely elegantly, but almost. He dances as I imagine he boxes, where every move seems to have a purpose. "This is great!" he yells, as though he's never yelled before.

"Kyle," Catty beckons, my head resting on her lap, "come over here." He sits a few feet away, just the right distance for me to rest my legs on him.

"Are y'all going to leave again?" I ask.

"Do you want us to?" Catty asks back.

"No, I don't."

"I ain't ready to go nowhere. I fell apart real bad this last time. And Kyle's all heartbroken about being his age and looking back and being nostalgic about it all. We ain't in no condition to get back out there, back to our lives. Whatever is out there will be out there when we return."

Meg seems stunned to have made her way up. Suddenly Catty yells, "Let's dance!" And we all stand and dance completely uninhibited, like we are performers in a tangled ballet on some important stage.

I feel accepted, more normal, dancing along a gray billboard, all of us singing "Sweet Jane" like we own it. We are the most glamorous thing the town has ever missed the opportunity to see. Up here, we are the entire night, making a dilapidated billboard electric. And I never thought of myself as beautiful, but tonight we are all stunning. Even Mastroianni and Kristofferson and Yoakam would approve.

When we are worn out, we sit back down and Kyle passes the bourbon around, with none of us taking anything more than a small sip. The music from down below has stopped. The night is quiet, and I love how it sounds right.

Meg, who for obvious reasons dances less and seems more pensive, overtakes the silence. "I've been afraid to climb up here all my life, so now that I'm up here I want to say something."

"What, honey?" Catty asks, reaching over, touching her hair.

"I'm going to have a baby," Meg admits. "In four or five months, I just want y'all to know that I don't need y'all to do anything for the baby. I'm going to take care of it. But I want you to know that I'm pregnant with our baby."

"Our baby?" Catty asks.

"Well, it was conceived that night in the diner when Boz passed out from telling the truth. I don't know whose it is, Kyle's or Boz's." She turns to Catty. "Or yours. You don't have to do anything, or even talk about it, but I'm having our child."

"Our child," Kyle says. "Everybody slept with everybody that night," Kyle says, informing me of what I can't remember. It is what I have not wanted to admit. When you lose yourself in that much lovemaking, you can't be sure of anything.

"Shit!" Catty says, standing up. "All that matters is Meg is having a baby and Kyle shoots big blanks. Sexy blanks, but blanks nonetheless. So it's Boz's."

"It doesn't matter," I remind her. "You knew what you were talking about when you said it was all of ours. You are right. Something happened in that diner that led to this. This just proves you were right. Meg, you always knew it was all of ours. You never said it was Kyle's. You knew."

Kyle is holding Meg on one side, I am on the other side of her, and Catty's holding her left hand. "Things happen, Meg. We can't explain them all. These are the best things. The unexplained stuff. Magic."

"Kyle, are you sure about your condition?" Meg asks

one final time.

He refuses to answer her. Instead, he says, "Meg, I'm glad we're having a baby. We are all having a baby!" he yells, his voice echoing across the river.

We get up and dance a final dance for the night, all of us thrilled about having this baby on the way. All of us, except Meg, who still seems upset. We pull her, as she is in tears, close to us.

Meg cries out, "But I don't understand!"

The music is loud, so looking at Meg seriously, I yell over it. "You will never understand. It will never be explained. Stop this. You got what you wanted, all of us are the parents of your baby!" Catty and Kyle are listening to me and Patti Smith and I think they are shocked that I am yelling at Meg. "Stop this!" I say to her again.

She does stop crying, though I know she is still perplexed. On the way home, she still looks a little worried, but not as frantic as she has been. On the short drive back, she falls asleep in the car and we carry her to bed.

That night, we all sleep with our hands somewhere near her belly, protecting her.

"I feel like it's my own," Catty says.

Meg sleeps straight through the night. We all love her more now, but loving someone like Meg means worrying more. She thinks we are worrying about the unborn child. Instead, she is the child we are still most worried about.

24

"I want to re-open the diner," I tell them a few days later. We are sitting outside on the steps, fanning ourselves, though the temperature has thankfully gone from ninety-eight to ninety-two.

"Boz, you're out of your mind," Catty has to say first.

"Maybe," I say.

"But all the customers, they won't come. You made the whole town mad at you," Meg reminds me.

Kyle is the only one not questioning me. Instead, he sits, silently listening, like maybe he actually thinks it is a good idea.

"It's not those customers I want," I say. "The Tavern has all those people late at night and in the early evening. We could liven the place up, make them want to come here."

They don't say anything, which, of course, I take as a sign of disapproval. "Boz, you're never going to leave this town, are you?" Catty asks.

"Maybe not," I confess. "That's why I want to make things better. I was thinking that maybe y'all could be part of it."

None of them want to look at me. They ignore me, as if I'm offering them to be part of something that will hurt them.

"Never mind," I say. "I'm doin' it."

I go into the diner and picture what can be done: how I can repaint it, put up some neon signs, make it come to life. It isn't that I can't do it without them, it simply seems less exciting and more like a case of me alone again, dreaming.

I don't mention it again. But late one Sunday, Catty comes

storming into the diner where I am taking some measurements of the baseboards. "Can I be the person that walks around making sure everything goes smoothly?" she asks.

I look at her to see if she is joking, but she is looking at me with the same seriousness I've seen her hold in important moments. "You mean the manager?"

"Well, I'd be good at that," she says.

"I don't know, yet. None of you have to be part of it at all," I say.

She pulls me close. "Honey, I wouldn't do this out of obligation. I'm thinking it could be fun."

As the days pass, I get more ideas about the colors I want to paint the place and the music I want on the jukebox. Meg and Kyle come around. "I want to be the head cook," Meg says one night in bed.

"Big surprise," Catty says.

"What do you mean?" Meg is offended.

"Nothing, honey," Catty says, reaching over, kissing her. "I just know how much you enjoy feeding other people."

I know I can make this happen. It is for real. Leaving Noxington no longer matters. Staying begins to not only make sense, it feels good. With them, I can stay forever.

"Kyle's good with money," Catty says. "If it wasn't for him, I'd be flat broke."

"Then Kyle can be the one who keeps track of the money," I say.

"Fine," he says.

From that night on, we spend all our time examining the diner, discussing things such as changing the menu to repainting the sign out front. Suddenly, it is an idea nobody wants to let go of. For me, the diner has become a sacred spot, a church for those who hate church. We look through online catalogs, keep the jukebox roaring, take more measurements, and make sure that this diner will be reborn. I've never thought of it as dead, but now I have them on my side to help wake it up again.

At night, we sleep all entwined, our arms, legs, chests, and backs all find their perfect fits in the bed. Because of Meg's condition, we move carefully during the night so we won't hurt her. This isn't at all a completely safe way of protecting the baby, but she insists on sleeping with us, having grown afraid to sleep alone.

"If this baby can happen like it did," she says one morning as she peruses a cookbook in the kitchen, "then anything can. I don't think a little nudge in the night is going to harm whatever is inside of me."

"A baby is inside of you," I say. "Why do you keep talking as if you have something completely unknown going on inside of you?"

"I guess it's because I don't care," she says. "I could never love this baby more than I love the three of you."

"But you'll still love it. Remember how you felt when you first touched your stomach, knowing somebody was in there."

"Barely," she says, flipping through the pages, not wanting to discuss this.

It is going to take some time for us to get the diner going. Almost immediately we find ourselves arguing over stupid things like paint colors or whether the coffee should be served in mugs or cups, but mostly it is Meg and Catty who fight over such things.

Kyle and I have been watching them go at it for days now. They are fighting about things, which only weeks ago they talked gently about. Their tone, when speaking to each other, becomes aggressive. They are now competing with each other for everything.

Kyle is growing more silent by the day. Catty and Meg go from fighting about whether or not to use paper placemats to fighting over who used whose lipstick or mascara. They are fighting like true lovers now.

I know that if they can just have the bed to themselves for a night, they'll stop this. But they seem to have forgotten how to make that happen. Though it is my money, my diner, I still value their ideas about the food, the décor, what the menus should look like. I believe that with the four of us, we can turn what has become our sanctuary into a profitable business.

Kyle breaks away during these days. Several times, I find him sitting in my bedroom window looking out down below. "They're at it again, huh?" he asks.

"Oh, yeah. Catty wants blueberry pancakes on the menu and Meg thinks it's a mistake since she plans on making blueberry muffins."

He laughs and shakes his head. "I guess that's how people who love each other talk."

Sitting down beside him still makes me nervous. I felt so close to him a few weeks ago, and now it feels as foreign as it did in the beginning. "Have you ever loved anybody that much?" I ask him. "Like Catty and Meg?"

"I don't know," he says.

I want to tell him how quiet he's been lately, tell him that I am worried about him, but can't find the words. That's why I raise his yellow polo shirt and touch his scar. It still feels good and warm. I know he likes it because of the way his eyes glaze over. This is a language we can both speak without ever uttering a word.

I don't want to stop touching him, but I have to get back downstairs before Meg and Catty kill each other.

"Thank you," he says, "for touching me again." He pulls at my hands. I start to walk away.

"I keep thinking y'all are gonna get mad about something and leave. I keep wondering why would two people with big lives in the big world stay here for so long."

"We stay here. We stay because of you. Because of Meg and the baby now. But in the first place, because of you. That is what you do to people, Boz. It's a powerful thing you got. You got a beautiful gravity about you."

Downstairs, I don't hear any yelling, so I think they must have exhausted each other with their arguing. Or that one of them has yelled at the other one to the point where there is some crying involved.

Instead, I find them in the kitchen. On the floor, their mouths are deep inside each other's legs. They make ecstatic sounds that echo through the kitchen like a love song recently rediscovered. For a few moments, I watch them be beautiful together and smile because they have found what they've been craving.

I leave them alone. I am relieved, knowing that the louder they get in the kitchen in this moment, the quieter they'll be about everything else.

25

None of us goes to bed at the same time these days, as everyone is working on his or her own aspect of the diner. But when we all finally make it to bed, Catty and Meg are pressed together more firmly than usual. I want everything to be like it was when we were on the billboard, dancing. I want us all to touch and be touched equally.

This changes in the way we all touch at night, leads me to work later than the others. I also enjoy the quiet of the diner, as I repaint the baseboards a darker blue. Catty fights with me about this color and I end up agreeing with her. "We don't want it to be just warm, we also want it to be vibrant," she tells me.

I don't really know how to paint, but am teaching myself as I go along, and it is working out fine. The diner is going to happen again. Kyle startles me when he walks in. "I can't sleep, and it's two A.M.," he says.

He strolls over to one of the tables and sits on it. "Boz, the more pregnant Meg gets, the more afraid of us she seems."

"I know," I say, trying not to look at him, not wanting to be turned on. "I think maybe it's a female pregnant thing. It'll pass."

I keep painting, pretending he isn't nearly as important to me as he actually is. Kyle has a way of rejecting me without even realizing it, so I pretend I don't care too much.

Even when I can tell he is watching me, I focus on something else. He isn't going to love me the way Catty loves Meg. Or the way that he once loved Catty. And he isn't even going to love me the way I think I can love him.

"Boz, will you touch my scar again?"

I stop painting and stay scrunched down by the baseboards, uncomfortable, unable to move. Then I remember how great he felt, so I say, "Take off your shirt."

He lays his shirt across the table. "Like before," he says.

I turn off the light so I can see the glow of the scar. "I see Portugal, but I always see Portugal on you."

"My great-grandfather was half-Portuguese," he informs me.

"I love looking at the world on your belly," I say. "But sometimes, I need to touch it and you seem reluctant."

"Why don't you ask? I love you touching me there, like it's the whole world." I do touch it like that, as though it is a precious porcelain globe. "I want this a lot of times," he says.

"Then why don't you ask?"

"Well, you know. Two guys. . ." he says.

"Yeah. We're probably wrong for this."

"I don't know about wrong, it's different for me," he says.

"No, it's not. You just think it is." I kiss his scar, licking it longer than I ever have. This time I see him hard through his boxers.

"More," he tells me. "Boz? Do you want me to touch your scars for a change?"

"I don't have any."

"The ones on the inside," he says. "Those are the ones I want to touch."

I am scared, thinking of him as a sensitive boxer, but a boxer nonetheless. We are both naked, and he places me on my stomach across the table, kisses my neck, and says, "I won't hurt you."

As long as he touches my scars, I don't care if he hurts me or not.

With his hands on my shoulders he enters me and it is so painful that I push him out.

"I'm hurting you."

"No. Do it again."

The second time hurts but I start to like it and he does reach my scarred insides. I raise my left leg to make sure he can reach all those wounded places inside me. He gives me a massage with his dick that makes me give off a short sigh, then I cry out.

"I told you I would come back to you," he tells me, as he drills into me, roughly kissing my neck. He is pounding me so hard I cry out, biting my lip. "I will always come back to you," he says, blowing his load. Afterwards, we crash into a booth and hold each other.

"Are you ashamed that you like to fuck men?"

"I like to fuck you, Boz. Not all men. You." He is almost whispering.

We fall asleep there, naked, clutching each other in a booth, never going upstairs that night to join the other two. However, on future nights, when autumn turns the nights cooler, when we are all in bed, we have more sex. Catty and Meg make love alongside Kyle and me, but we all touch. Sometimes when Kyle is deep inside of me, when I am feeling pain that I have needed to feel all my life, I reach over and grab Meg's hand as her head is between Catty's legs. And I find myself with him inside of me, arching my back so I can reach Catty's lips to kiss her hard and with everything I know how to kiss with. Passion is not lacking in this room these nights. Kyle learns to like having a dick in his mouth. He says it makes him feel like his mouth is full of possibilities.

Catty and Meg have their own routine in which Meg's breasts are the focus. For the first time in ages, it feels right again, with all of us loving each other in just the right way.

I'm still not sure if Kyle is completely okay having sex with me because sometimes during the day, he spaces out, like he is even more troubled than usual. But knowing he loves me some is enough.

And after these foursome nights, we still go down and have our breakfasts. Also, Meg is happy and she is trying out various new recipes. On a morning when she is baking a chocolate chip cake that she is sure will be a hit with our future customers, she falls over in pain.

The baby isn't due for another three months, but we all pile into the red car and speed along, taking her to the hospital.

Scared to death, none of us says a word on the way. Except for once, when I turn to her as she squeezes my hand, and I say to her, "You'll be fine, Meg. This is probably normal."

26

I've never spent much time in hospitals, so they fascinate and frighten me, the doctors being paged over intercoms, all the white coats, and a smell so clean that it is dirty are all things that freak me out.

"It's the baby, I can tell," Meg says. "I've never felt this before." She is all pale, breathing hard, looks dizzy, like she is going to collapse or like the baby is trying to punch its way through her navel. In fact, as we enter the sliding glass doors of the small hospital, I expect to see something small and alive to march right out of her stomach.

Some of the workers stare at us through glass windows. A heavyset, perky young nurse who looks younger than Meg arrives. I am struck by the way she smiles, like she serves ice cream for a living instead of sometimes welcoming those who arrive with more blood outside than within. The nurse doesn't ask what's wrong at first, so I blurt out, "She's pregnant. She's in pain."

"How are far along are you, hon?" the nurse asks her.

"She's almost six months," I say. "She's in pain."

"Are you the father?"

"No," I look around. "Well, kind of."

The nurse looks puzzled as more people surround Meg, bring out a stretcher, and put her on it. We all breathe hard, like we are also in need of medical attention.

They start wheeling her away behind those swinging doors with those small topsy-turvy windows and those god-awful white-striped lines, which form diamond shapes all around.

Kyle and Catty and me all start towards the doors. The pleasant nurse still has a calm, content look on her face but says, "Y'all can't go back there. Not all y'all. Only the father."

I look at Catty who is scared white and Kyle who is nervously pacing around like a lost dog. We are all frozen in that way I freeze when I can't see the future at all.

"Who's the daddy?" the nurse asks again.

"I am," Catty says.

The nurse smiles, thinks it's a joke. "Are you her sister?"

"You could say that," Catty snaps back.

I can hear Meg's voice coming from somewhere behind those doors, short sharp wails. I want to be diplomatic, want to be fair about all of this, but I barge through the doors like a daddy.

"Boz," Meg says, clutching my hand as they hook some bags up to her and give her some sort of shot.

And for a brief moment, I see the pain leave her as a look crosses her face like she's dead enough right now to never want to die again. There is fiery regret in her eyes, the wish that she hadn't spent her whole life not wanting to be here. Because now, even though it's just because we're all scared, it seems like she can die. I don't know anything about childbirth, but I do know that such pains are probably not a good thing.

"Am I dying?" she asks the aides, but they don't answer, so she turns to me.

They push right past me like I'm one of the ghosts I keep in my room. I am invisible as Meg disappears beyond some more of those doors that feel like they hit me each time they swing.

These are doors that can snap fingers right off or cut a person in two, which makes going through them seem so final.

Then there is the same nurse again, with her hand on my shoulder. "You might want to go out there to be with your family," she says, thinking we are blood relatives. She sounds even farther away than those nurses whose voices keep coming in over the intercom.

I stagger to the waiting area and I must look bad, crazy-tired at least, because Catty and Kyle move to make space for me in the torn blue vinyl chair between them. They wrap themselves around me, each of them placing a single leg over my own. We are the only ones in the freezing cold emergency room in the middle of nowhere. And we warm each other, ignoring the way the nurses, the custodians, the doctors look at us.

Catty holds my hand, strokes my hair. Kyle's head is on my shoulder. There is a television hanging high from a corner wall. An LSU game is on. I know that being in this middle chair is as safe as it is going to get this night.

I only get up once after we have all fallen as asleep as any person can in a hospital waiting room. And when I do, I go to the overly lit bathroom. Once inside, I walk over to one of the sinks and splash some cold water on my face. I don't know what this is supposed to do. I only do it because I've seen it done in the movies and this seems like the right time to try it out. I look at my wet face for the longest time in the mirror, the drops of water scattered all over it. It feels good and I do it again, then again. The final time I wet my hair a little, then I wet it completely.

I want to see what will happen next. I expect to either see

an image of Meg in a coffin or one of her holding a baby. I am used to knowing these things beforehand. I wet my face one more time, like the wetter I am the more I'll be able to see the future. But I see nothing. Instead, I just shiver and dry off with the hand-dryer and some of the coarse off-brown paper towels hanging nearby.

When I go back out, they don't say a word about me being damp. They just make the same spot for me in between them. They've managed to get a blanket from somewhere and Catty yells out to a passing nurse, "Hey, honey, can we get a towel?" Ignored, Catty gets up and walks through the doors she's not supposed to walk through and returns with a small white towel. She dries me off. "Boz, you are beautiful," she tells me.

We lay there under the blanket, waiting for news about Meg. We cling to each other, fall in and out of sleep. We turn these uncomfortable chairs into an indoor campsite and make a home, refugees crossing some frozen border of an unfamiliar country.

27

Morning happens. Meg is still alive. And so is something that resembles a newborn baby. It is not long after we see the baby that we begin to wonder why he survived.

I want it to look different from other babies, like he has four parents. You know, like that it has Meg's nose, or Kyle's mouth, or Catty's eyes, or my eyes. But it doesn't.

The only thing that makes it special, besides the fact that we have created it, is that it is more than two months premature. And small. So small, in fact, that I think that it's one of those babies who will die. But this tiny baby is kicking and moving around with great force, like Kyle at the punching bag.

I want to love the baby. I want to be thrilled. I want to feel warm and feel the joy of having a newborn baby that I have helped create and come to life, but I don't. I don't feel much of anything. There's something so natural about the fact that he has been born. It simply feels like it is what is supposed to happen on this day in Noxington.

They have the baby in one of those rooms where so many babies are, the ones who have some problems like holes in the heart, only half-functioning lungs, or have simply been born too early.

I expect Meg to be weary. After all, she has always been the lively yet worn-down type. But in the room, she is glowing, even more so than when she was pregnant. She is propped up in the bed, in some pain, but not really showing it. She has been in hospital beds so many times that she operates the bed position controller with great expertise.

Catty and Kyle are standing by me as we make our places around the bed. Meg is all full of energy, like she's had too much iced tea or jellybeans, neither of which is allowed right now. "The doctors say he's going to be just fine," she says.

Catty takes her left hand and kisses it. "Well, he'll be fine. How are you feeling?"

"Great. Just a little sore, but you know, I've been worse." She looks around the room with a quickness that surprises us. "This is kind of exciting. I've never been in a hospital bed without being treated for something to do with being depressed, or not depressed, or sad or whatever. It's not so bad in here."

"Things will be okay, Meg." Kyle takes her other hand.

I don't think the baby is beautiful. I don't think much of anything about the baby. I know this is supposed to really be a moment, but I don't feel enough.

"Boz?" Meg asks. "Why don't we name it something cool? Something dreamy. After a movie star or singer or somebody we've always wanted to meet."

"I don't know," I say. "I don't know what to call it."

"You promised you would name it. Remember, you wanted to."

"I know," I say.

"Surely," Catty jumps in, "you must have thought about this."

"I have," I say, "but I'm still thinking."

"What are some of your ideas?" Kyle asks.

"I don't know right now," I say. "Can I think about it for a while? Why does it have to have a name so soon? Can't we wait a day or so?"

"I guess," Meg says.

"Maybe if I go look at him again, I'll think of a name." I get up, none of them trying to stop me. I can feel they're excited. I can see by the way they are grasping Meg's hands, the way they are looking at her, that they have that warm, whatever feeling you are supposed to have when a baby is born. I have to get out of the room.

I start towards the nursery then turn around. There is something that makes me not want to be here. There's something I can't see in the baby that I am supposed to see. Something I can't feel. I have no idea of what is going on with me. I find my way down one hall that leads to another, nearly crashing into a short lady wearing a hairnet and pushing a tray full of food. Like all hospitals, there are exit signs everywhere, but it's so hard to find my way out.

I am dizzy, sicker than Meg seems to be right now. I stumble to the light I see coming from what looks like an exit. Once outside, in the cool air, I shiver, having left my sweatshirt inside. I feel like I do when I try to leave Noxington, but I'm just leaving the hospital. I grab onto a rail, people are scattered around, but I don't care. I can't stop myself from bending over and letting the sickness out. The confusion hits the ground and I keep my head hanging there, out of sickness, out of not wanting to get up. I wipe my mouth and feel less dizzy.

I need to go back in there. At some point, I will, but right now, I just have to walk. I have to get home to my room, to my sanctuary, to my place of solitude, the easiest place to be until they all moved in. This is the first time that I have felt the need to be away from them. I need to go back to another time, just for a moment. I need to stop some traffic, watch an Italian movie, and listen to Kristofferson.

I stagger a bit, drunk on the new day. I keep walking, past the hospital, past the truck stop, past the church, past everything. In my mind, I am somewhere else, on a beach in California, on a mountain in Switzerland, a bar in the French Quarter. I am everywhere but Noxington.

I run awkwardly up the stairs to my place. Inside, I don't put on music or a movie or anything. I throw myself on the bed. I cover myself with every pillow and blanket and sheet I can find. I am buried beneath faded purple and green pillows and sheets, and the threadbare paisley comforter. And I let the silence beat me up. And it feels good. Just nothingness again. In this room where everything has happened, I just lay still and take in the pain of the silence that surrounds me, knowing that it won't last for long.

I don't cry, but I drift off wanting to. It's like I've never been alone in this room with the silence before. For the first time, it's not the same. It's overwhelming. I don't even want to be in this room.

When I fall asleep, I want Granddad to wake me up talking to me, or one of those movie star ghosts to visit me. But nothing, nobody comes to me. I am left with restless half-sleeps of Meg and the baby. And how I hate it that she's had the baby. When I awake, I want it all to have never happened.

When I finally dig myself out of the pillows and sit up, Catty and Kyle are there. He sits on the side of the bed, and she lies beside me.

"What happened?" Catty asks, "What's wrong?"

"I don't know," I say. "I wasn't feeling well."

"Are you upset about being a father?"

"Are you?" I ask back. "We're all the parents, remember. We all did this."

"You make it sound like a bad thing."

"You said you never even wanted to have a baby," I say to Catty.

"Oh, honey, but one is here. When it happens, you have to adjust."

Kyle lies on the other side of me. "How do you feel Boz?"

"I feel like I don't love that baby," I say slowly, knowing that I am telling more about myself than I want to. And I don't stop. "I kind of sorta hate that it's been born."

"Oh, Boz," Catty says.

They snuggle on both sides of me, becoming new pillows. "Meg wants to see you. She's worried about you."

Then the tears come, not a lot, but just some that slip out when I blink. "I just don't love that baby," I say.

"You will," Kyle says, wrapping his arms around me as Catty kisses my tears. They both smell like a mix of sweat, hospital, and sweet cologne and perfume.

I don't believe him, I don't know what to believe, but I'm not dizzy anymore. And I am glad that they are back. Silence in a run-down room in a small town just is not what it used to be.

They hold me and kiss me until darkness comes, believing that if they hold on long enough, I will eventually make it back to the hospital to see Meg and the baby.

28

Over the next few days, I don't learn to love the baby, but I do learn to stay at the hospital longer, to hold the baby, to not hate the baby. When something is that small and helpless, it's really hard to hate it. But most people have an easier time warming up to their newborns than me, I guess.

"What's the name?" Meg wants to know.

"What's the rush?" I ask.

We are sitting in her sunlit room. The nurse is there, watching me with caution as the baby grabs at my fingers and moves around a bit, always semi-sleeping. "It's a beautiful baby." The nurse looks longingly at this no-named son as though he's the only one she's ever seen.

"Catty and Kyle went to some store in Slidell to buy some new clothes for the baby," I tell her. "They said they'd be here later."

Meg is smiling. It is around noon on a Thursday. Meg is staring out the window with a look on her face like she is just discovering the world. "You know," she says excitedly, "we'll be going home soon. The doctor says he's doing so good. I mean, they'll probably wind up sending me home first. Mama and Daddy came and are afraid that I'll go home too early and get all crazy and stuff. But I feel fine."

"I love the sun in the fall," she says. "When we are in the middle of blazing summer, I often think that it's never going to come again. But it always does."

The baby seems comfortable with me, and I am getting used to it. Maybe you learn to love babies the way you learn to love people. Perhaps it doesn't happen all at once.

"Boz, when you are finished with the baby, let's go for a walk. I want to go up to the cafeteria. This is only the second day I've been allowed to do that."

"We can go now," I say, as the nurse reaches and takes the baby. Meg kisses him goodbye, as she makes her way out of the bed, still a bit sore.

I help her fasten her nightgown. "These things never fit," she says. "Who cares who sees what?" she adds.

I help her tug along her IV as we make our way out of the room. "You have to lead the way," I say, "I always get lost in here."

This day, Meg looks more beautiful, more radiant, than she has in years. It's like she's found something in herself that she didn't know she had. I wonder if she knows how stunning she has become these past few days, how alive and sane and strong she is. "You look good, Meg," I tell her. "Better than I have ever seen you."

She stops. "Really? You mean that? I don't look all bloated and stuff? Are you sure? My hair is a mess."

"It's perfect. You are perfect," I say, putting my hands on her shoulders before pulling her close.

We get to the elevator and go up to the seventh floor. The elevator is empty and quiet, and this moment with her is so good that it makes me want to just stay on it for a while. But we get out on the floor where the cafeteria is. "I don't want to go in there right now," she says, "it's too crowded."

"Well, I know you don't want to eat anything."

"No, you know I don't need food. But I like the smell. Even of cafeteria food." She takes my hand, and leads me, as I hold onto her intravenous drip.

We make our way to a sitting area where there is an elderly man on a cell phone. "The chairs in here are kinda comfortable," she says. "And I love the way the light comes in. Like in your place. It's just right."

Meg opens one of the windows. "Somebody will complain that it's too cold, but I need to feel that air," she says. We stare ahead, like we are really looking at something, like we're on a cruise and have a room with a view of the ocean or an exotic city. In reality, the only thing below us is a parking lot full of pick-up trucks and cars that carry the sick and those worried about the sick.

"I love you, Boz," she says, her hand in mine. "Why did you run away the other day?"

"I don't know why."

She rests her head on my chest, taking in the air, "You were angry, you didn't want the baby. You thought you did, but when it came, you couldn't handle it."

"It was just overwhelming, that's all."

"Well, you'll learn to love it more and more," she says. "It will love you back."

"I know." I say this, hoping it's true.

"Remember before they came?" she asks.

"Yeah."

"It was so dull around here. And now look…" She laughs a little.

"You are really happy about this baby," I say.

"You know why I'm so happy," she says. "It's because all my life, I have never done anything right. Ever. It's always been halfway done. He's premature, but he's going to be fine." She rubs her fingers along my arm. "You know, I dropped out of the community college three times, couldn't work for my dad or anyone else, never learned to eat, couldn't get the hospital stays just right." She looks straight at me. "But this time," she says, "I got it right. For the first time, I did something right. I gave birth. This is something that I never thought I could do. That is why I'm so happy. When you've been doing everything wrong forever, it feels good to know that you've had one time when you've been accurate, when you've done something just the way it should be done. Something right. I never knew it before, but that's all I ever wanted."

I pull her close, kiss her on the head. "Meg, you are something. And yes, this time, you got it right. You really did something. Something beautiful. Dwight Marcello is something only you could create."

"Dwight Marcello. That's the name. As in Yoakam Mastroianni?"

"Well, yeah. But because my name is on the birth certificate, it's Dwight Marcello Matthews."

"I love it," she says. "Now it's complete."

We sit quietly for a while, getting a chill from the window, but Meg seems to like it. "Aren't you getting cold?" I ask.

"A little," she says, getting up to close the window. She stands there looking out at the parking lot. "When are Catty and Kyle going to go back?" she wonders.

She turns to look at me. I smile at her because she's standing there like she's really figured it out all out. She's finally got the look of a woman instead of a girl. A woman who knows who she is, and who knows what life is about. She is all lit up by the sun. And she is so content that she is beyond smiling. She's beyond words. She's found joy, and I catch a glimpse of her glowing eyes. There is nothing more amazing than Meg, fully alive, in the sun in autumn. Even though she's attached to the IV, I get the feeling she could just take it from her veins and be fine. She doesn't need anything except the light and the cool air and the notion that's she's done something right.

"Oh, Boz," she says, the sunlight almost engulfing her, "we are really something, aren't we?"

I suppose we are.

29

I am asleep in between the two of them. I've begun to take my place here. Right between Catty and Kyle. It's an amazing place to be. Each night, while Meg is in the hospital, our hands find their way all over each other and we end up making some sort of new love. Sometimes it's me sucking Kyle's dick while his tongue finds a home between Catty's legs. Or sometimes it's Catty's mouth on my cock while Kyle fucks her. Or him fucking me, or whatever. We're at the point where the only thing that matters is that we are together, and that there will be room for Meg when she comes home.

On this night, a Saturday, we are all lying here, knowing that tomorrow Meg will be returning home. The baby will come shortly thereafter. I know that things will change. But this night after we fall asleep to George Strait, and we wake around five A.M., Kyle does what he has done before. He fucks Catty, then me, then Catty, then me again. Later, I get up and walk to the window. Outside, the air is autumn cool.

I feel wide awake, knowing Meg is coming home tomorrow. I look around the room, which is filled with tons of baby stuff, clothes, a stroller, toys. Now it doesn't bother me that there will be a baby coming home. I want us all to be together.

I pull on Kyle's jacket, the worn-out denim one that I like to wear and that he doesn't mind me wearing. "Where are you going?" Catty asks.

"I just want to be outside," I say.

This night, before everything changes, I sit on the rickety

stairs of the diner. I think of Granddad, of how I miss him, of how he never comes to me anymore, not in my lightest or deepest of sleeps. And I miss them first arriving, the beginning of it all.

I don't know what it is about this night that is keeping me up. I haven't been up late nights walking the streets or the diner for a long time. Certainly not since Meg went into the hospital. I am now sitting on the pavement in front of the diner, which we need to continue to work on so that it can have a grand re-opening.

"Counting the trucks?" Kyle asks.

"You scared the fuck out of me."

"Sorry. I thought I would." He wraps his arms around me tightly.

"Not really counting them," I say.

"Then what's keeping you up?"

"I can feel it," I say. "You can really feel it," I say. Change is in the air."

He's never held me like this. "When I first left Noxington, I thought I was going to miss this peaceful nothingness."

"Did you?"

"Not until you."

We sit there and stare at the cars and trucks that pass by. There are only a few, but I can tell that he used to dream of getting away, and that there were many nights he sat wanting to run away. "You're brave," I say.

"For what?"

"For getting out."

"Oh, Boz," he says, pressing his gray sweatshirt against my

back. "It's easy to leave a place you don't like. Staying in a place you don't feel right in. That takes guts."

"Then I guess we're both tough," I say.

"Well, I knew that about you all along."

"It will be different when Meg comes home tomorrow, won't it?"

"Yeah."

"I'm not saying it's gonna be bad, just different."

"Yeah," he agrees.

I feel his breath on my neck and think of Catty sleeping soundly upstairs. "Boz, you know there's one thing that tough guys do. I have never done it."

He takes my hand and leads me into the diner. I still don't believe that men can really get away with this around here, but somehow we have been able to so far. Inside, in the half-refurbished diner, he starts to take off his clothes. I don't get undressed. I just pull out my hard dick through my fly and watch as he spreads himself across the center booth. I don't worry about anyone seeing. He wants it so bad that the whole world should watch.

I spit on my hand, and because he wants to feel tough, I don't worry about if it's going to hurt too much. He wants it to. He cries out and lets out something of a laugh at the same time. He moves against me. "Is that all right?" I ask.

"It feels so good," he says.

I let him have it the way he gave it to the punching bag or to the guys in the ring. He lets it all go for me. It's like I can beat him up now. I can hurt him, but I'm not, I'm making him feel something brand new. "Harder," he says.

And I fuck him more across the diner table, drilling him like I've never fucked or been fucked before. The table is slamming against the wall. I want it to last forever, but he pushes back and comes all over the placemats.

I find myself letting go inside of him. He takes a moment to steady himself. Then he throws himself into one of the booths. I turn around, zip my fly. And there is Catty sitting in her nightgown against the wall. She is smiling.

"Oh, boys," she says. "You didn't think I was going to miss that one."

I walk over and sit down beside her, resting my head on her shoulder, feeling like she is glad she saw Kyle give in, glad to see him somewhat defeated in the booth where he is still trying to regain his composure. When he stops breathing hard, he gets up, slips on his underwear and comes over to sit by us on the floor.

"We have to finish working on this place," I say.

I relax in between them, thinking about Meg coming home tomorrow, about what has just happened, about what I am capable of, and feeling love like I have never felt. Feeling a toughness I never knew skinny guys like me who can't drive cars or ride motorcycles or fistfight could ever feel.

30

By eight A.M., we are already at the hospital. We are tired from the night before, but have learned how to survive on sex and little sleep. It's one of those rare days in Noxington where you can either wear a sweater or not. The temperature is just right, the sun is just right, and the sky is so blue it seems like a mistake.

We pile out of the car at the hospital. We make our way through the sparsely-crowded parking lot, and through the sliding doors. "You think she'll be ready?" I ask.

"There'll be paperwork, we'll be lucky if we're out of here in two hours."

Catty and Kyle have dressed well for the occasion. In a tight blue dress, her makeup and hair looks like she's about to go on stage. Kyle's wearing a tan blazer with a gray T-shirt and jeans. Me, I'm just wearing an old Alabama T-shirt and some khakis.

The doctors, nurses, aides, have all become used to the freak show they think we are. They can't quite figure us out. "You know they talk about us," Catty says.

"I hope so," Kyle says, as we near Meg's room.

She's holding the baby when we arrive. "Two more days, she says. Me today and the baby in two more days. Boz, Mama was here earlier. She says hey. Daddy's new church is doing real good."

For some reason, maybe it's the clear blue sky, or the way Meg looks at me, but I walk over and take the baby in my arms. He has grown twice as big as when he first started out.

"He's gonna be fine," I say.

"Damn straight," Catty chimes in, taking him from me.

The nurse in the room, Carolyn, has gotten used to tolerating us, though she's a church person who never approves of anything much. Kyle sits in a chair and starts flipping through a copy of *People* magazine. "Can't they hold the baby while I go talk to the people in the business office?" Meg asks the nurse.

"I guess so. The daddy is here," she says, rolling her eyes.

"That's right," Catty says, "your daddy is right here," referring to herself. "Singer Catty Mills becomes proud papa. That makes both of you proud mamas."

"I can live with that," Kyle tells her.

I channel-flip, trying to find something to grab my attention on the tiny television hanging above. Catty sings to the baby, Kyle starts reading *US Weekly*, I fixate on *Good Morning America*.

"It's time for him to go back now," the nurse says. "I'll have to have him back."

"Only two more days," Catty says, as we gather around and send the new prince back to his tiny, glass-sided, soft bed.

"This always takes forever. Her parents are paying for this. What's the hold up?"

"Catty, how many hospitals have you been in? You know discharging takes forever."

Catty walks over and sits on his lap. "Forever is a long time, baby."

They kiss quickly on the lips, until a young woman dressed like she's ready to take the census comes in. "I'm looking for

Miss Richards."

"She stepped out," I say.

"Well, when she comes back, tell her to come to the billing office."

"Oh, honey," Catty says, "she's at the billing office."

"Well I haven't seen her there."

"Maybe she talked to someone else," Kyle says.

"I'm the one at the front desk. She didn't come in."

It hits me right then, just like I know the woman on *The Price is Right* is going to win the new car they've just shown, just like I knew Granddad would be dead, just like I knew the baby would be fine. I know. I can see it so plainly it might as well be on the television screen.

I jump.

"Boz?" Catty is alarmed. "Boz?"

I start to walk, faster, then faster until I am running to the elevators. "She's on the seventh floor," I say to Catty and Kyle as they trail behind.

Elevators are never there when you need them, but this one is. I jump in and close the doors. I try to re-open them for Catty and Kyle, but hit the close button instead. And when the elevator stops, I run to that place, to that room where Meg feels most comfortable. I look around, but she isn't anywhere to be found. All the seats are vacant.

Meg can vanish like this.

Just as I am about to leave the waiting area, I see her, standing there, in the window she loves so much. She has one hand braced on each side of the window, the sunlight is coming in. Megan Richards against a blue sky on a sunny day is simply gorgeous.

She is hanging there like she's been there her whole life. A window fixture. A human curtain. She is as yellow as the sun. "Meg," I say. She doesn't say a word. She is no longer with us. No longer part of this world. She has gone to some other place. I walk towards her but stop, knowing that my hand will simply go right through her. She is untouchable. She is not here, not really. Only the body she never really needed is here.

Her eyes are aglow, the only thing about her still part of this quiet town, this world. And she looks right at me. She is a blaze of some sort of glory. Her eyes do the talking. "You promised," she says. "You promised."

I hear the elevator open, I hear Catty and Kyle coming down the hall. There are others. I hear their voices. I go closer to her and she steps back, hanging in the air for a few seconds. She walks into the sun the way some people walk into the ocean. Just a step back and then they are no longer there. She hovers. Catty and Kyle rush to her. I didn't know people could hang in the air like this. Not even Meg. The hospital workers, security are all around now, and Meg disappears into the sunny day. She knows where she is going. It is time for her to return to that place where bodies aren't necessary and food does not exist.

Catty stands as still as Meg had been. Kyle wraps his arms around her. I wrap myself around Kyle. We huddle together, holding each other.

When someone like Meg is ready to go, you let them. After all, she was already gone. A person can't match the sun and sky like this without being ready to become part of it. Besides,

I know that you can't stop someone from doing the thing they have always wanted to do, at the happiest moment of their life. She wanted to disappear while happy. People leave. And you have to let them go.

31

The baby is still in the hospital, and we worry about him. Even me. I can't say I love him the way I should, but I am thinking about how small he is and how something so small deserves to be thought about more than anything else.

We are restless and move around the room like there is a pocket of comfort somewhere and we are all searching for it. For a while, I lay on the carpet, then I crawl into the bed with the two of them, then I'm back on the floor. They do the same thing, but at different times. We aren't moving through our choreographed sleep the way we usually do.

I finally see the light coming in through the window. Morning feels good when you see it happen sober. Before I met them, I mostly saw the morning when I was drunk and sad and lonely after a night at The Tavern. But now, the sun coming up is the most dependable thing in our world.

"I love the sun. In the morning." I say, feeling like I haven't slept at all. I crawl in bed with them, as they are moving from the very edges of the crumpled sheets to be near each other.

"Sleep has never been so hard," Catty says, getting up, naked and smooth in the sun. She is digging through every pant pocket and crevice in her purse. "I thought there might be a Valium in here. I know I spilled the bottle in here one day."

Kyle rises, all naked and almost bearish in the way he gets up and stumbles to the bathroom. I hear him peeing. "We should get on the road early," he says. "The funeral is at ten."

"You know," Catty says, lying back down, "if Meg were alive, she'd hate to go to such a funeral."

"We have to go," Kyle says returning from the bathroom.

"I didn't say we don't," Catty said. "Boz, you all right?"

"I'm okay," I tell them. "Just couldn't sleep again."

"I love you." Catty says coming over to me on the floor and laying her head in my lap. "Now that Meg is gone, you're what we have left."

"You have each other," I say.

"Yes, but we've had each other forever," she pulls on Kyle's fingers. "Ain't that right, Kyle?"

"That's right."

We still haven't cried about Meg. "People around here don't die normal deaths," I say. "Nobody except Granddad died the simple way. People around here die differently than in other places. I don't know why that is but they do. I wish that they went out in other ways. You know. Simpler, heart attacks or common cancers. People around here die like they want you to know they are going away."

"I knew it was coming with Meg," Kyle tells us.

"She was slowly going away over the past few weeks," Catty says.

"She was going away her entire life," I remind them. "There was something so natural about it," I say. "Only Meg could jump out of a window and make it feel like she died of natural causes."

I wear some of Kyle's clothes, because they are nicer than mine. In the bathroom, as the light flickers above the sink, Catty and Kyle straighten my black tie against my white shirt.

"I don't want to look too pretty," I tell them.

"Too bad, Boz. You're already pretty," Kyle tells me.

Kyle's wearing a less-white shirt and a navy blue jacket and pants. Catty is in the black dress that she was wearing the first night I met her.

In the car, we don't say much. Voices come from the national public radio station. The calm broadcaster might as well be talking about another planet. Wars and bombings and the stock market are things that happen somewhere else.

I lounge in the backseat as Kyle puts on a hard rocking oldies station where "All the Young Dudes" is on. When I had first heard this song, I thought I would conquer the world.

We are soon on the Causeway, the twenty-four-mile bridge across Lake Ponchartrain. There is a great deal of traffic, many SUVs and suburban folks heading to work. It's more sophisticated the closer you get to the Causeway, then New Orleans.

I am thinking of the baby, my baby, our baby, wondering if he'll be the next funeral. There have been so many of them this year. Another one wouldn't surprise me.

The water along both sides of us sways and ripples with the wind. In a while, we will enter a funeral home full of dressed up New Orleanians. I will feel out of place. I will not want to look at Meg, but I will. And I will want to wake her up.

We take our seats in the back of the place, which smells like flowers, but I try to think of the smells of Meg, of Coca-Cola lip gloss and French toast. I am sitting in the middle, and we all hold hands. We have become somewhat used to being thought of as faggy or weird or whatever. I can't be anywhere but with the two of them right now. Their hands mean a lot to me.

The preacher preaches. It's that preacher who has his own TV show on the public channel. I always find him good-looking. He's all solid and rugged, full of power and lies, and has a booming voice. He is Pentecostal, and I don't want to listen to it. But I do. He's talking about how Meg is in a better place, as if we hadn't figured that out. But I can't listen entirely when my heart is beginning to break. Catty and Kyle just stare at the ground. I look straight ahead, waiting for Meg to get up and walk over to us.

When it is all over, I know that there will be her family to talk to. I know that there will be lawyers at some point. I know that her parents will want Dwight Marcello. And I'm not sure that I don't want them to have him.

But after the sermon, instead of talking with anyone, the three of us get up and move toward the coffin the way Meg would have. We walk like we are only sort of there. Sort of somewhere else. Sort of untouchable.

At the front of the huge room, which must have had nearly three hundred people, it's like we've learned to be in places and not be there at the same time. People leave you alone when you are like this.

They've pulled Meg's hair back. They've put on makeup. She looks beautiful, but nothing like the natural gorgeousness I knew as Meg. People are moving all around us, and we stand and stare.

"Boz," Meg's mother says, coming up from behind me.

"Not now," I say. "Not now." I say this quietly and turn to look at her. Mrs. Richards looks all puffy like she's been crying or taking some pills herself. "We loved her so much," I say. And I know there will be awful legal stuff to deal with, but for now, for this moment, it's like she believes me. Like she understands.

On the Causeway, on the way home, the clouds have rolled in. The only thing we can hear is the rain. We haven't been this silent since we've met. The rain is our conversation, our music. I look out past the water, at a boat in the distance and wonder why they didn't stay on shore with the waves and winds picking up. I wonder who would take such a small boat out in such dangerous weather.

Catty's voice starts up. She does what we need. She sings "Farther Along" like I have never heard it before. She kills me more than Gram Parsons, more than The Byrds ever have. In the backseat, I start to cry a little. The world has turned gray and white and black with flecks of every color of every car that passes on this long bridge. Catty carries on, her voice keeping rhythm with the rain. Kyle joins in and sings.

In the distance, the boat is still there. It might capsize, it might be okay. I see Meg waving from the front of it. I round my hands like binoculars so I can see more, and I am sure that I can see her there on the boat, in one of her light green summer dresses, holding out a jellybean for me. A girl I have to believe is Meg is across the water staring at me, then waving.

For the first time since she jumped to another world, I start to cry harder. My words hurt coming out. "It's just so beautiful out there today."

32

My room now is now a nursery. Near my Merle Haggard poster is his crib. Near my whiskey bottles is a stack of baby formula. Then there are the red, green, blue, multi-shaped toys that he's not even old enough to care about yet. "I think we should start going to the place in Mandeville more. Staying there," Catty says softly. "More room for all of us."

"What about the diner?" I still have not even seen the place in Mandeville. The only thing I know is that it is on the water and Kyle finds it too fancy.

"We can come back and get the diner started."

Catty gently lies Dwight Marcello down to sleep. It is beautiful to see some tiny living thing so full of fighting and screaming drift off in the softest way.

I walk outside to the staircase and sit down, wondering why Kyle is taking so long to get formula. "Catty," I ask, "Do you think he's going to be okay?

"What do you mean?" She follows me outside and softly pulls the door closed.

"I mean, you know, damaged? His brain and stuff. The doctors said you can't completely tell until . . ."

"Don't talk like that, Boz. He's fine."

"I'm not sure, I'm just . . . what if he's not?"

"Boz!" she says, raising her voice, before lowering it. "Who cares? He's your son. Besides, a few flaws will just give him character."

"I don't want him to be brain-damaged; I don't want him to be somewhat slow, or to walk differently."

Catty's arms around me now. I feel her breast against me through her tight blue T-shirt. "Shhh. . . everything is fine," she says, breathing on the back of my neck, kissing my right ear, biting it a little, getting me hard. "It's been a while since we've done this. Just relax, Boz," she says.

She moves along the rickety stairs of the outside of my place, of our place, and unzips my jeans. I am hard for her. I need this. Her mouth always feels like home. I lie back and she continues to make love to my cock, to me. "Catty," I say, "It feels so good."

"Give me some," I hear Kyle say. "I want some."

He leaves the shopping bags at the bottom of the stairs and stomps up to us. I close my eyes, and then watch them, these two beauties while they both work on my hard cock. It's as if they need to lick my cock and wrap their mouths as much I need them to. They are hungrier than me.

While Catty licks one side and Kyle licks the other, they are almost kissing each other, with my cock being a third tongue that they are fighting over. Kyle pulls my jeans down, and then my white briefs to below my waist. He starts to lick my balls while Catty keeps sucking me.

Then Catty reaches beneath me with one of her long fingers and slides it into me. It hurts, but I love things that hurt in one place and feel good everywhere else. But I don't expect Kyle, in his brown leather jacket, corduroys, and boots to also reach under me and stick another long finger, only thicker, inside of me. I hold the noises somewhere deep in my throat. As they lick me, suck me, and find places inside of me with their warm fingers, I start to shake. It's that good.

I start to buck against the stairs. They aren't touching themselves, yet their eyes seem like they are the ones about to come. I didn't know these stairs could handle such weight and action and pressure.

The whole staircase is shaking. I see the sky, and hope that God, some god, is watching this. I hear my voice about to break. I hear the staircase creaking. We might be breaking it. Somebody could be watching. This is dangerous. This is love. This is wonderful.

Because I can't hold either the soft yell in my throat or my load anymore, I let go. The whiteness that comes out of me seems to hang in the air for a few seconds before zigzagging in various directions. The sky seems to be coming closer. Catty and Kyle take turns kissing me, then each other, then me again.

"You gotta let it out sometimes, Boz," Catty says.

"You're learning to like it rough," Kyle tells me.

"Thank you," I say, having never been fucked by a man and a woman at the same time like that. It's amazing to be with people who know exactly what you need.

"Let's go get cleaned up," Kyle says. "Are we still going to The Tavern?"

"Sure," I say following them to the huge bathtub where we quickly take turns washing ourselves and each other.

As Kyle and I put on our boots, the baby stirs, but he doesn't wake. Catty has drifted off in the new rose-petal painted rocking chair.

Kyle and I try to leave as quietly as possible, knowing how hard sleep is to come by. We also know that you can be as forceful as a hurricane and yet barely make any noise at all.

33

The Tavern is packed tonight. "Last month there was a rumor that John Anderson was going to come perform. He wanted too much money," Hazel says, as Kyle and I sit at the crowded bar. "We can't afford those big Nashville stars. No offense, but we could barely afford Catty Mills."

"Offense taken," Kyle says, raising his beer bottle.

It's all jukebox tonight, all dart throwing and foosball and pool. The place is full of everyone who's gone wrong at some point. I feel at home.

Hazel serves a couple of cowgirls on the other side of the bar. One of them, the one with the long dark hair, winks at her, and I think maybe they are like us. I am finally beginning to be able to tell when people are open in that way.

"So they didn't hassle you about the legal stuff?"

"No. I'm shocked, but no. Meg's mother said, 'He's your son.' I think it's because he's not perfect. If there was a chance that he would not be damaged, then they would be wanting him."

"To your son," he says, raising his bottle, grinning, looking like someone you love is supposed to look when they smile.

"Our son," I say.

"Our son," he agrees. "Dwight Marcello."

Hazel comes over to us. "Get this. . . the one on the left just asked for my phone number."

"Good."

"But my phone got disconnected yesterday. Tips have

been bad. I didn't pay my bill. Shit. What should I do?"

"You'll just have to tell her to come back in to see you. Tell her that you don't give out your phone number to the customers. Tell her you'll get fired. That you're not allowed to."

"See, Kyle, Boz is so good at this stuff."

"Is it true that y'all are moving to Mandeville or New Orleans?" she asks Kyle. "Are y'all going to take him away from here?"

"We don't know yet where we are going to go. But we can't stay here forever. We have to get back to work and stuff. We were hoping to get the diner up and running again, but the baby, you know, sort of threw us off track," he tells her.

She scurries away to wait on some of her other regular customers. I've had a couple of shots, but don't want to get too drunk. I don't know where we are going to move or end up living. I don't talk about it much with them. They sometimes fight about it, and even when they are arguing over where to live, I know that they will end up choosing the right place.

There are a few couples dancing on the floor. I recognize some of them from church. "They must have backslid," I tell Kyle.

"We all do. Some people stay slid, though. Like us."

"Sometimes," he says. "But there are times when I want to be like everybody else."

The Marshall Tucker Band comes on. "Heard it in a Love Song" is played here several times a night. And I never get sick of it.

"You're proud of that, aren't you? Of staying slid?" I ask him.

"Sometimes," he says. "But sometimes I want to be like the people who go to work, get married, have kids, retire, die."

"It's hard for you to be back here. Back home?"

"It was at first. But after a while all that hurting that you feel just wears you down. When you grow up in a place like this, but you live in big cities and see the world, and meet all different types of people, it's hard to feel like you're one or the other, a city slicker or a country boy. When it comes down to it, nobody ever wants you to be two things, to play two parts."

I drink up some of my beer. "When do you feel like you want to be like everyone else? Does it happen a lot?"

"Just sometimes. Most of the time not."

"Like when."

I want another shot of whiskey, but I am worried that I might cross the line and get drunk and get into a fight with somebody or something.

"Like, you know, now. I wish that I could go over there with you. And we could dance with the others." He picks up my shot glass and motions for Hazel to bring us two more. "Even with Catty. You know, she's sorta famous, so I can never be like everybody else when I am dancing with her."

"And I thought you loved being different," I remind him.

"I do. But I have my moments. There's always this thought that you will wake up one day and be comfortable with exactly who you are. And the older I get, the more I feel like that, more comfortable, but I'm still not there."

"Here hons," Hazel says. "It worked. Look at her. Her hair

is so long, I told her she looked like Crystal Gayle."

"She does," I say.

"Tell her to come over here," Kyle says.

"No way, you'll embarrass me."

"I won't." Instead of waiting, Kyle goes over to the cowgirl and starts talking to her.

"What the fuck is he doing?" Hazel asks.

"I don't know."

The woman gets up and comes over to me. She does look like Crystal Gayle, except her eyes are a little smaller, and she is thinner. "Your friend told me that you want to dance with me."

"Hazel will get jealous," I say.

"It's not that kind of dance," she says, "Hazel has nothing to worry about."

She takes me and leads me through the crowd, to the corner of the tiny dance floor. We begin to sway slowly to "Old Flame" by Alabama. Kyle shows up with three more shots of whiskey. He stands behind this cowgirl and we make a sort of sandwich out of her. I miss Catty.

But before the song even ends, Hazel's crush slides away and starts dancing with her friend who has also come over. And now it's just me and him. He takes my hands and he pulls me close, a little drunk, a little brave, a little backslid.

"How does this feel?" I ask him as he presses against me.

A few people are watching, but they don't take us too seriously, and think we're joking around.

"It's good," he says. "I love you, Boz. And it feels fine."

After the song, he kisses me on the lips.

"I don't want us to get in a fight with anyone."

"Catty's gonna be mad she missed this," he says.

"I know," he says, looking at his watch. "I told her one of us would be back by now."

"I can go."

"No," he says as we stand still in the corner of the dance floor. "You gotta play matchmaker for Hazel. I'll go."

I walk him out, and watch him get in the car. I don't argue about going with him, though I'm not sure I want to stay much longer. But I have to let him go home.

Back inside The Tavern, it's getting rowdier and the Hank Jr. music is louder. And the cowgirl is cozying up to Hazel at the bar.

I look around. Just like at Meg's funeral, I am able to be in this room full of people and yet barely be here. Before I met Catty and Kyle, I would have been looking around, fantasizing, wondering who the people in this bar are. Wondering if there is a beautiful stranger somewhere in the room. Wondering if I am a beautiful stranger. Wondering if there might be something here that could plug me in to the rest of the world and keep me charged.

Tonight, I don't know what to do with myself. I now have the ghosts I desire. It's all okay. It was never supposed to be like this. I wasn't ever supposed to be able to stop after three shots of whiskey. I was supposed to go crazy or go to jail or to have simply died by now.

As I walk out into the night, I feel alright. Like maybe everything is more than okay. Almost perfect. I am full. I am done.

I start the walk home. Walking along the side of the road, I see a pick-up truck. Unlike before, this time, I don't fantasize about stopping it with a direct look. After all, that person deserves to go wherever he or she wants.

When I get back to my place, I creep up the stairs where I was loved earlier. It is as silent as it's been since the baby came home. And I don't want to wake any of them.

Catty and Kyle and the baby are sound asleep. Kyle must have come home and passed out because he's still in his boots. Catty, of course, is half-naked in one of her always-open robes.

Catty is lying on Kyle's chest. Kyle's right hand is stretched out and is hanging over Dwight Marcello's crib with a tiny stuffed light blue cat in his hand. This must have been how they all fell asleep.

Everything is flawed in this world. There is something wrong with everything. But not this. It is exactly right, the way they are all breathing together, the way they are finally sleeping, the way the posters of my recent younger years blend in with baby bottles, boxing gloves, and photo albums of faded Nashville stars. I have never done anything right, not really. And I've certainly never done anything this right.

This peace, the perfection of this ancient room being filled with exactly what it always needed to be filled with, is so powerful to me. Having never seen something this right, this correct, I am afraid that if I breathe too much or too hard, or walk too loudly or too fast, I will ruin it all.

When you see something this good, you have to make sure

it remains that way. Again, some things you just have to leave alone. When you've helped create something like this, you have to move away from it before you start destroying it.

So this is the night that I quietly go to the closet and get what I should. They will not understand at first, but someday I hope they will. Perhaps they'll never fully understand my decision because they can't see what I see right now in this darkened room in a nowhere town at three A.M.

After my small duffel bag is packed with a couple of extra T-shirts, underwear, and jeans, I take the money from the can on the top shelf. Everything in this moment is the way it is supposed to be. I am supposed to leave them alone. Alone to move to Mandeville or wherever they will start living their lives again.

I don't need to walk over to look at them before I go. This image is already a photograph that is burned into me for the rest of my life.

I walk down the stairs for the last time. These stairs will stand forever.

I wait for that feeling, that dizzy feeling, that nausea to come on. This time, I intend to puke and keep going. If I have to, I'll faint my way to wherever it is I am supposed to be going.

But sickness doesn't come.

A blue and yellow eighteen-wheeler slows down. I don't know who is in it. I don't know where the truck is headed or where I will end up. I have done something right. I deserve to be leaving. And I am.

Thank you to Bill Contardi, Gabriel Levinson, and Thomas Keith for believing in this book.

ABOUT THE AUTHOR

Photo by Brian Trzeciak

Martin Hyatt was born just outside of New Orleans. He attended Goddard College and Eugene Lang College of The New School. He holds an MFA in Creative Writing and is the recipient of an Edward F. Albee Writing Fellowship and The New School Chapbook Award for Fiction. His stories have been published in *Lodestar Quarterly, The Electric Literature Blog, Blithe House Quarterly*, and several award-winning anthologies. His first novel, *A Scarecrow's Bible*, published in 2006 to wide acclaim, won the Edmund White Debut Fiction Award and was a finalist for the Violet Quill Award, the Lambda Literary Award for Gay Debut Fiction, and the Ferro-Grumley Award for LGBT Men's Fiction. It was an alternate featured selection of the Doubleday/Insight Out Book Club and was also named a Stonewall Honor Book finalist by the American Library Association. *New York* magazine declared Martin to be a literary "Star of Tomorrow." Martin teaches creative writing at various colleges in the New York City area. He is currently completing a memoir entitled *Greyhound Country* and lives in Manhattan with his husband, physicist Massimo Porrati.